HE SAYS:
"I resent everything you want out of marriage that I've already had. And for making me reach so deep inside to give it to you again."

SHE SAYS:
"I'm not Barbara. And I'll be damned if I'm going to recreate *her* life just to make *my* life with you work. This is *our* life now . . ."

....AND THAT'S WHEN THE GAME BEGINS
IN NEIL SIMON'S
BROADWAY AND HOLLYWOOD SMASH HIT

Chapter Two

Now a novel by Robert Grossbach

NEIL SIMON'S
Chapter Two

A novel
by Robert Grossbach

Based on the screenplay
by Neil Simon

WARNER BOOKS

A Warner Communications Company

WARNER BOOKS EDITION

ISBN: 0-446-92279-X

Warner Books, Inc., 75 Rockefeller Plaza, New York, N.Y. 10019

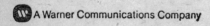 A Warner Communications Company

Printed in the United States of America

First Printing: April, 1980

10 9 8 7 6 5 4 3 2 1

FOR MY DEAR MOTHER, MOLLIE SIMON,
AND HER NEW HUSBAND, HY

1

The big plane was tracing rings around Long Island the way children circle an answer in a picture-book exercise. Over and over, for a half hour now. A holding pattern.

Leo will be crazy, thought George. The flight was already forty minutes late, and Leo couldn't stand to wait ten seconds. George chewed frantically on his Bubble Gum and resisted the temptation to blow a bubble. The plane slowed perceptibly. It was almost time to switch fantasies. Airplane trips were a continual source of disaster images for George, starting with a flaming crash on takeoff, through ditching at sea, through running out of fuel during the landing delay—and then an agonizing earache on descent that left him permanently deaf. It was to avoid this last horror that George chewed the gum. Barbara had always said—He cut short the thought, concentrated instead on life without hearing. He looked across the aisle, tried to read the lips of the man and woman sitting there. Impossible. Occasional words came through, but that was all. George felt like crying. Lost—the world of sound. Forced to read the accompanying sign language on TV laxative commercials, never to be awakened by the perpetual pile drivers that hammered outside his apartment from 7 A.M. on—and never to hear himself applauded at the National Book Award ceremony for author of the Best Novel. Of course, that wouldn't happen anyway. That was one fantasy George didn't have. He was a writer, yes, but a first-rate author, no. An active imagination was one thing, thought George. Delusions were another.

The rows of lit-up Queens houses were clearly visible out the window now. George was glad it was nighttime; somehow, during the day, the area looked much bleaker, dismal: large patches where shingles were missing from the roofs, forlorn children looking up and pointing. . . . But the darkness cloaked everything, reduced the life below to a pretty abstraction. George's ears were clogged. In rapid succession he visualized coming down on the Belt Parkway, the plane's tires blowing out as they touched the runway, a small, private craft smashing into them as they taxied to the terminal.

"Thank you for flying Pan Am," announced the stewardess as George unbuckled his seat belt and stood up.

"No matter how many times I fly," said a man next to him in the slowly moving line of passengers, "I'm always glad when we finally get on solid ground."

"Really?" said George, hearing the man's voice as if through a faulty long-distance phone connection. "I never think about it myself."

He straggled into the International Arrivals building, holding his trench coat over one arm, and headed for the baggage area. Fifteen minutes later he was amazed to see his two blue suitcases emerge on the circular treadmill. He'd expected them to be lost. He snatched each of them up in turn and headed toward the customs lines. Six separate queues had formed; he ran toward the shortest one. Ahead of him, a black woman in a turban was having her luggage virtually dissected. The luggage was a disheveled array of cloth sacks and paper bags, and the contents, ranging from erotic-looking underwear to bunches of bananas, were strewn all over the inspection table. A second officer was called over, and then a cart was brought, the sacks and bags piled on, and the woman led away. She made no protest, seemed to take it philosophically. George wondered what had been her crime. Were the bananas illegal? Or was sack-and-bag luggage deemed improper for anyone entering America?

"Next," said the inspector.

George placed his suitcases on the table.

"Anything to declare?"

George shook his head. He handed the inspector his blank declaration slip. The man motioned for him to unlock his suitcases. George fumbled with the keys. *Unbeknownst to him, the black woman had managed to slip two kilos of pure heroin into his bags, street value ten million dollars. Caught, he'd be sentenced to thirty years in federal prison, while authorities announced "major drug bust."*

". . . been away?"

"Huh?" said George. The customs inspector was looking at him peculiarly.

"I said, how long have you been out of the country?"

"Oh . . . sorry," said George. "My hearing. . . . Uh, I've been out three-and-a-half weeks, not counting the flight." He grinned.

9

The inspector remained stern. "And you have nothing to declare?"

"No."

"You bought nothing in three and a half weeks?"

George hesitated. He envisioned the hand signal to the second inspector, himself being led away, his luggage in the cart. "I ran out of toothpaste once," he said. "That's about all."

The officer ran a meaty hand through the chaos of George's second suitcase. Without Barbara to pack for him . . .

"You can close them," said the inspector tonelessly.

George nodded gratefully, snapped the lids shut, and headed for the arrival area. He was more than an hour late; Leo would be apoplectic.

A large crowd had gathered behind a heavy steel railing. George paused and looked around. Suddenly, he heard someone calling.

"George! Hey!"

A medium-height, fortyish man wearing a raincoat pushed his way through the crowd.

"George, over here!"

George stood face to face with his brother, Leo.

"Hello, George."

"Hello, Leo."

For a moment, the men just stared at each other. George tried to smile, but found himself holding back tears. Finally, Leo embraced him tightly. They stood there, hugging amidst the hurrying streams of humanity.

"Watch out for pickpockets," said George when they had finally separated.

"Always worried," said Leo. "My big brother always looks out for me. One second back from across the ocean and he's worrying about them picking my pockets."

"You don't think it can happen? Especially you, you carry your wallet in the back."

"I have a sensitive ass," said Leo as they headed toward the exit. "I would feel their fingers. Besides, I keep a plastic statue of Karl Malden on my dashboard."

Outside, the cool night air was refreshing. They trudged across the parking lot. Low flying planes droned overhead.

"I still have some residual hearing," said George.

"What?" shouted Leo.

"I said I still have some hearing, even after the landing."

"Well, I don't!" yelled Leo, as a 727 appeared to land almost on the roof of his Oldsmobile. He opened the trunk and tossed George's bags inside. "So what was it like?" he asked.

"What?"

Leo pinched his lips. "What, he says. Playing Johnny-on-the-Pony with Margaret Thatcher. Your *trip* I'm talking, dummy. Europe."

"Oh, that." George was imagining being mugged in the parking lot, then the cops finding the Olds vandalized, torn to shreds, battery stolen, transmission dropped. . . .

"How was London?"

George looked up. "Full of Arabs."

"Yeah, I heard it's all changed."

"Not all. The Rosetta stone is still in the British Museum. The Elgin Marbles."

11

"Oh sure, yeah, I remember those. I used to play immies myself a little." Leo laughed, and lightly punched George's shoulder.

George had spent seven days in London, trying to get the feel of it again, visiting all the tourist places, even just sitting and feeding the pigeons in Hyde Park. In the end, it was still depressing.

"They say Italy's gonna close in two weeks," said Leo as he walked around to the driver's side of the car, entered, and reached across the seat to open the door for George. But George remained outside, staring vacantly at the sky.

"Aren't you gonna get in, George?"

George nodded dazedly.

"That's why I came to pick you up," said Leo. "So you could get in." He started the car, and George opened the passenger side door and slid inside.

"You lost weight, didn't you?" said Leo.

George patted his stomach. "A couple of pounds."

"Sure. Who could eat that lousy food in Paris and Rome?"

George smiled. Leo had no appreciation of food whatsoever, no taste, no discernment. Often, at expensive restaurants, while everyone around him was ordering chateaubriand and asparagus with hollandaise sauce, Leo would demand a cheese sandwich and wolf it down as soon as the waiter brought it.

They headed for the exit of the parking lot, where George insisted on paying the bill.

"My brother the sport," said Leo.

"Where else for two bucks can you buy eternal gratitude?" said George.

They drove into the maze of roads that criss-crossed the airport. "There!" said George, spotting a sign. "Take that one. It leads to the Van Wyck."

Leo nodded. He was a lousy driver, not alert, frequently lost. "So where'd you stay?" he asked.

"Well, in Paris I stayed on the right bank, a small hotel off the Champs Élysées."

"Nice?"

"Not bad. Except the mattress had a depression like a meteorite had landed. When I woke up after the first night I discovered I was a quadruped."

Leo pulled onto the highway. "And Rome?"

"I stayed in a *pensione*. Also not bad. The bathroom had no toilet paper, but otherwise it was fine. I had an excellent view of the Communist rallies from my window."

"I thought I'd take the Belt to the Battery tunnel," said Leo.

"Take the Van Wyck to the Long Island Expressway," said George. "This time of night it's only jammed."

Leo nodded. "So," he said.

"So."

"So d'ja meet anyone interesting?"

"Like who?"

"What do I know like who? The Ayatollah Khomeini."

"We hit different parties."

"Then anyone. A person. A girl." The highway lights flickered off the planes of Leo's face; he looked like a figure in a silent film.

"Nope."

"No girls left in Europe, George?"

"I didn't see any."

13

"Did you look?"

"All I saw were a lot of guys who needed shaves."

Leo exhaled sharply. "I think you could have used a vacation on your vacation, George."

"Don't rush to judgment. Inside, I'm a new man."

"You look tired."

"It was too expensive to sleep there."

They passed the American Airlines terminal, where a small crowd had gathered in front. "Glad I'm not part of *that*," said George. "Arrive in the middle of the night and first have to fight your way into a cab." He shook his head. "Terrible. I feel sorry for those people."

"They're paying for past sins," said Leo. "They didn't think to arrange adolescent victimizing by younger brothers, so that those same guilty siblings would later in life feel compelled to pick them up at airports."

"You mean you're here out of thirty-year-old guilt?"

"Certainly. What then? Even though it wasn't my fault that I was the loved one, while you were only the smart one."

"I always thought *you* were the smart one. Maybe your grades didn't show it, but on intelligence alone, down deep, I knew you were tops."

"You should've told my teachers that."

"I'm planning to write them tomorrow," said George.

"Oh, nice," said Leo. "Maybe they'll change my marks." They were on the Van Wyck Expressway now, moving north through the center of Queens.

14

"So all in all, it sounds like you had a pretty good time," he added.

"I had a shit time," said George.

"That's what I said. It sounds like you had a lousy trip."

"Ah, the whole thing was foolish," said George. "I should've known before I started."

"Known what? I thought the idea was to get away, take some time for yourself, not visit the same places you went to with . . . you know . . ."

George turned to face him. "Barbara. Her name was Barbara. You're allowed to say her name, Leo."

"All right. Barbara. Anyway, why didn't you go to Norway or Sweden? They got no ugly girls there, they send them to Finland."

"The worst thing would've been to go to Europe looking for girls," said George.

Leo shrugged. "I'm not sure I follow that, but I'll accept it if you say so."

"I was doing perfectly fine till I got to Rome," said George. "In Paris, I even saw a woman throw up right on Napoleon's coffin. The guard fined her two francs on the spot for 'fouling zee tomb.' I was doing really well, and then one night I took a walk in one of the piazzas, and I saw a middle-aged couple kissing near a fountain. Can you imagine? My age, and they were kissing in the street."

Leo stared straight ahead out the windshield.

"That's when I got angry with Barbara," George continued. "I mean furious. I said, how *dare* she go and die on me? How *dare* she! I would never do that to her."

"I can imagine what—"

"You can't imagine, Leo. You really can't. I was like a nut, walking up and down the Via Veneto, cursing my dead wife."

"In Italy they probably didn't pay attention," said Leo.

"In Italy, they agree with you," said George.

●　●　●　●

Back at the American Airlines terminal, among the people who weren't being met by guilty siblings, was Jenny MacLaine, returning from her divorce. Thirty-four years old, pretty, in a drained, pale sort of way, she stood next to her friend, Faye Medwick, in the line wating for a cab.

"Taxi!" called Faye musically. "Yoo-hoo, here. Taxi!"

"It doesn't work that way," said Jenny. "You just have to wait in line for them. It's not like in the streets."

"I'd like to wait in line, if I could only find it," said Faye. "At this point, a line would look good to me."

"There's a cab shortage," said a man standing in front of them.

"Really?" said Jenny. "I guess I better stock up."

"Job action by the drivers," continued the man. "Supposed to last only one day."

"That makes me feel wonderful," said Jenny.

Faye tapped her on the shoulder. "Should we stop off at a grocery? Your refrigerator's probably empty."

Jenny shook her head. "I dropped an order off with Gristedes before I left."

"Before— You're having them raise a cow for you?"

"They were supposed to deliver the order this morning. We'll soon see. . . ."

A cab pulled forward, but the man in front of them, instead of entering, held open the door. "Ladies. . . ."

"You're kidding," said Jenny.

"I'll get the next one," he said, smiling.

Jenny and Faye smiled back. "I'll be dipped," said Faye. They entered the taxi, and the man slammed the door.

"You're a gentleman and a sweetheart," said Faye out the window as the cab pulled away.

"Ask him if he's married," whispered Jenny loudly.

The cab driver turned his head. "Chwhere to, ladies?" He was a Latin with pockmarked skin and several gold teeth.

"Twenty-first and ninth," said Jenny. "Manhattan."

The driver narrowed his eyes. "Chwhere's tha'?"

"You don't know where Manhattan is?"

"Oh chure, I know. It's the other part."

"Just get us to Manhattan first," said Jenny. "We'll direct you from there."

"I still can't believe it," said Faye. "You fly two thousand miles to get a divorce and you remember to leave a grocery order?"

"It's that Catholic upbringing. I majored in discipline."

Faye pulled out a small mirror and began to redo her makeup. Faye was *always* redoing her makeup. When she was done, she found Jenny staring out the window. "You don't *look* any different," she said.

"Well, your features don't actually change until the final papers come through. Then, I believe a scarlet letter 'D' slowly emerges on your forehead."

"I'm glad you haven't lost your sense of humor," said Faye.

"I lost some of it," said Jenny. "The lawyer took a third."

A light drizzle spattered the windshield.

"If it rain chard, we chab to stop," said the driver.

"Why's that?" asked Jenny, not really wanting to hear the answer.

"No chwipers," explained the cabbie.

"You asked," said Faye.

"Never again," said Jenny. "I promise."

Faye put away her mirror. "I tell you, if it were me, they would have taken me off the plane on a stretcher."

"Well, that's one thing we'll never have to worry about, will we?" Jenny said.

Faye looked at her steadily. "Really?"

Jenny cocked her head. "Trouble in suburbia?"

"You make it sound like a soap opera."

"I just meant, it sounds preposterous."

Faye stared at the floor. "Sidney and I had dinner with friends last week. A couple married twenty years."

"That's depressing right there."

"There's worse. The man never stopped fondling his wife for a minute."

"Oh, God."

"They both said it was the best time of their

18

lives, that they never really knew how to enjoy each other till now."

"I'd have bludgeoned them on the spot."

"Know what I thought?" said Faye. "I thought: shit. Twelve more years to go until the good times."

Faye's eyes filled with tears. Jenny reached out and took her hand. "You know what, Faye? Yours was the best face I ever saw at an airport."

Faye forced a smile. Outside, the drizzle stopped.

"I think this our lucky night," said the driver.

2

The apartment house was on eighty-first street, just off Central Park West. It was a short walk to the Museum of Natural History and the Hayden Planetarium, and George would often spend weekday afternoons in one or the other, staring at the dinosaur skeletons or checking what his weight would be on Jupiter. He remembered going to the planetarium as a child, he clinging to his father, Leo held by his mother, the four of them awed by this fleeting, artificial contact with the majesty of the universe. Things had changed. Their father was gone, their mother moved to Florida. Leo said he had better things to think about than the universe. And George was a middle-aged man, hoping to recapture something—he wasn't sure what—by haunting a museum.

The car crept slowly up the street and came to a halt just as another vehicle pulled away from the curb. Leo clapped a hand to his forehead. "Am I hallucinating, or is that a parking spot that just opened up? I must be hallucinating."

"I believe it's a sign from God," said George.

"In this location it's a greater miracle than a burning bush."

Leo was backing up. "How'm I doing?"

"Cut! Cut! Cut the wheel!"

The Olds crunched against the bumper of the car behind it.

"You didn't cut enough," said George.

Three attempts later, they were parked. Leo ran around to open the trunk.

"First time," he said.

"That what? You parked in four tries?"

"First time in five years I found a space in front of your house. Maybe I should get an apartment here. I don't want to give up this spot."

They trudged inside with the suitcases. George stopped at the mailbox before they entered the elevator. Two minutes later they opened the door to his apartment.

"Whew!" said Leo, as they stepped inside. "This place could use a little air."

"I wasn't going to leave any windows open," said George. "The robbers in this neighborhood take the plasterboard off the walls. You're lucky if you have floors."

"Yeah, but it smells like the opening of King Tut's tomb." Leo put the suitcases in a corner of the living room.

George was sifting through his mail. "Occupant, apartment 6C. Occupant. Resident. Nice to know that somewhere, deep in the bowels of an IBM 370, I am loved."

"Which reminds me," said Leo. "Speaking of bowels. You know what I think it is? Gas."

"What?"

"Do you smell gas, George?"

"No."

"I think you left the gas on."

"Ah," said George, holding up an envelope. "Here's one with my name. Amazing what computers can do these days." He walked into the kitchen and turned on the light.

"Just don't strike any matches," called Leo, "or we'll *both* be back in Italy."

In the kitchen, George spotted the picture on top of the refrigerator: a photo, Barbara and himself, ten years ago, her arm around his waist, both of them smiling. It had been taken in the Catskills, at a hotel. Well, what was he supposed to do? he thought bitterly. Throw it out? Get rid of it like a pair of old shoes? He forced his gaze away, tore open the envelope.

"There must be a slow gas leak in the pipes," said Leo, coming into the kitchen.

"All of a sudden you have such a delicate nose?" said George. "You, who would rather have tuna-on-white than Szechuan beef with garlic sauce?"

"Just sleep with your windows open and your mouth shut. Try not to breathe much. What are you reading, by the way?"

George had extracted a note from the envelope.

"Strange," he said. "A letter of condolence."

"They're still coming?"

"I thought I answered the last one before I left," said George. He scanned the note. "Do we have an Aunt Henry?"

"*Aunt* Henry?"

"That's what it says."

"We have an *Uncle* Henry in Kingston, New York." Leo shrugged. "You want a beer?"

"This is signed 'Aunt Henry.'"

Leo opened the refrigerator door. "Uncle Henry's about sixty-three. Maybe he's going through a change of life."

George read from the letter. "Sorry to hear about your tragic loss. With deepest sincerity, Aunt Henry."

Leo reached into the refrigerator, sniffed, and grabbed a cardboard container. "You want to see sour milk?"

"I think you got cheese there, Leo."

Leo replaced the container, withdrew a yellowish mass. "You want to see white bread that's turned into pumpernickel all by itself?"

"Listen," said George, "I heard penicillin was discovered in the mold that grew on an orange. I ask you, can I do less?"

Leo extracted a shallow plastic bowl. "You want to see a dish of grapes that have dried into raisins?"

"What is this, a biology course here? Things change. That's the nature of life." He saw Leo looking at him. "Some people just can't adapt to it easily," he added.

Leo dumped the erstwhile grapes in the garbage.

"Leo?" said George.

"What?"

"Do you smell gas?"

Leo's eyes widened. "*Now* you first smell something? I think your nose is having jet lag, George." He found a can of beer in the back of the refrigerator. "I can't wait to try this," he said, pulling the flip top. "Inside, it's probably Scotch by now."

George placed the letter on the table. "What do you think I ought to do about this apartment?" he asked.

Leo took a swig of the beer. "If it was me, I'd sell it."

"Yeah?"

"Yeah. My suggestion? Move. Get out. Find a new place for yourself."

"I really love this apartment, Leo."

"All the more reason not to stay."

"I spent the best twelve years of my life here."

"I know. My opinion still stands."

They moved out into the living room. Leo sat on the couch, George paced back and forth as he talked. "It was really weird in London. I kept walking around the streets looking for Barbara . . . places, restaurants we used to go to."

"Georgie . . . don't torture yourself."

"I thought to myself, It's a joke. She's not really dead."

"George, you want some beer?"

"She's here someplace playing out this romantic fantasy." George walked to the window and stared down at the park. "The whole world thinks she's gone, but she's here waiting for me in some flat, and we both disappear from everyone and live out our lives in secret." He turned in time to see Leo shaking his head. "What are you saying 'no' to?"

"George . . ."

"She would have thought of something like that," George insisted.

"But she didn't," said Leo softly.

George stared at him, a shattered, bewildered expression on his face.

"*You* thought of it," said Leo. "It was you."

George came away from the window. "Yeah," he whispered. He sat down next to Leo. "So, my sweet baby brother, anyway . . . I'm back."

"I'm glad you are," said Leo.

"Chapter two in the life of George Schneider. I have writer's block with my existence. Where the hell do I begin?"

Leo puffed out his cheeks. "I don't know. You want to go to a dance?"

"A dance. My God! Medical students free, no doubt? Flatbush Jewish Center maybe? Door prizes?"

"No dance, huh?"

George grinned. "You know, you're cute." He pinched Leo's cheek. "Does Marilyn think you're cute?"

"It's not enough," said Leo. "I want *all* the women to think so."

George paused. "Everything is okay at home, isn't it?"

"Couldn't be better."

"You sure?"

"Hey. Never ask a question like that twice." Leo shrugged. "Want me to get tickets for the Knick game on Saturday?"

"Kinda late, isn't it? I mean all the good seats are probably gone."

"Oy," said Leo. "Mr. Naive. How many times I told you, I have important friends. In my business, people do favors. I know season ticket holders haven't been to a game in three years."

26

"I think some of the Knicks haven't been to a game in four."

"So. You want tickets, tell me."

"Who they playing?"

Leo rolled his eyes to the ceiling. "How should I know? I know from basketball? The Mets, maybe. Or Japan. I don't know. I tell you, for a guy who's gonna get something free, you're a tough negotiator."

George picked up another photo from an end table. A foursome. Leo, Marilyn, himself, and Barbara. The deceased, he thought. The deceased and I.

"George?"

"I'll let you know," he said quickly.

Leo shrugged. "How about dinner on Sunday? Monday? Maybe Tuesday will be my good news day?" He imitated the movements of a trombone player, then noticed that his brother's eyes were unfocused. "Hey, George?"

Again, George forced himself to pay attention. "I'm okay, Leo. I promise. Just give me a little time, all right?"

Leo nodded. "Now *I'm* mad. I really am. I think it stinks too. I'm not going to forgive her for a long time." He placed a hand on George's shoulder.

"Thanks," said George quietly.

"Listen," said Leo, "I'm coming back next week and the two of us are getting bombed, you understand?"

"Absolutely."

Leo stood up. "I mean, I want you dis*gusting*."

"No problem."

They headed for the door. "Then we'll drive up to Kingston and check out this Aunt Henry. If he's got money, he might be a nice catch for you."

George smiled and opened the door. Leo walked out into the hall.

"I'll lie down in your parking space when you pull away," called George. "That should hold it for at least five minutes."

"You take care of yourself!" Leo yelled back.

George watched him in silence until the elevator came. Back in the apartment, he noticed something: he still had his coat on, had never taken it off. That's what happens, he thought, when men live alone. They revert to infancy, or progress to senility. Wear the same underwear for four days in a row. Eat eggs and frozen pizzas for all three meals. Forget to sleep. Forget to wake up. *Not all men*, came a gnawing inner voice. *Only you.* He walked into the bedroom, removed his coat and threw it on the double bed. Leo was right, he realized. The place was impossible. Everything was built for two people, *screamed* of shared resources. He opened the door of the small closet, removed his jacket, slung it over a hanger. Alongside . . . *of course* . . . another closet.

Compulsively, his hand turned on the knob. Her wardrobe remained as she had left it. Undisturbed. *Barbara's things.* To give them away was unthinkable, as was throwing them out. Throw them out? *These were Barbara's. Barbara's.* She wore these things, they were close to her body. He reached out, touched the sleeve of one of her dresses.

"I'm still here, honey," he whispered.
How could he ever leave?

•   •   •   •

"Use your imagination, folks," the owner had said. "Think what you could do with this kind of a place."

It had seemed charming, renting an open floor-through in a brownstone, a creative challenge. Although her senses and intelligence and husband had all told her it was really only one big room selling for the price of three, the challenge seemed to stay with her. Admiring friends would marvel at her ingenuity and style. *Think what you could do with this kind of a place!*

As it turned out, not very much. Regardless of how many tricky dividers Jenny arranged, and how many area groupings she contrived, the geometry always seemed to predominate. The fact remained, no matter how you sliced it—it was still one large room. Friends nodded politely instead of marveling.

Faye stood at the window, looking out onto Twenty-first street. "There's a man outside," she said casually, biting into an onion bagel with cream cheese.

"Mmm," said Jenny. Gradually, she was clearing her suitcase of clothes, putting each item away as she removed it.

"He's doing something really degenerate."

Jenny stopped. "No kidding. Is he exposing himself?"

"Nope." Faye was tearing at the bagel hungrily now.

29

"Peeing?"

"Nope."

"Well, what then? Killing someone? Raping? Vomiting? What?"

Faye licked off a last bit of cream cheese. "He's painting someone's car."

Jenny crossed to the window. A well-dressed man in a three-piece suit was carefully going over a white Plymouth with a spray can of blue enamel. "He's not even putting graffiti on it," said Jenny. "He's just . . . painting."

"He's a neat degenerate," said Faye.

"Next, you'll be asking him if he's married."

The man stopped, took a few steps back to survey his work, then moved away.

"Another night, another paint job," said Faye. "Meanwhile, how about another bagel?"

Jennie returned to the suitcase. "Why don't you go home?"

Faye's eyes widened. "That's a very wonderful thing to say to someone who came to meet you at the airport."

"I just meant you must be tired, that's all."

"Jenny, relax. Let me worry about me."

Jenny shrugged. "You're not going to hang around here till I've readjusted, are you?"

"I like it here," said Faye. "I've always loved this apartment. It's small—"

"But spacious."

"Easy to take care of—"

"When cleverly laid out."

"And very sexy."

"Sexy?" Jenny laughed. "*Now* you tell me." She hung a dress in one of the closets.

Faye went to the kitchen alcove, cut a bagel in half, and buttered it. "So? Do you feel single yet?"

"Not as long as I can still smell the ghost of Gus's cigar," said Jenny. She strode into the bathroom, emerged with a can of air freshener, and sprayed at random around the room.

Faye sat down on a chair. "Don't deodorize my bagel," she said.

Jenny wrinkled her nose. "The thing is . . . a cigar. God, what a cheap item to be haunted by. When does that go away?"

Faye reached over to an ashtray and held up a cigar butt. "When you throw it out." She tossed it into the ash can.

"Why do those things remind me of dog shit?" said Jenny. "Why couldn't he leave a bottle of men's cologne around, or even some nice, aromatic pipe tobacco?"

"Maybe he intended to finish smoking it," said Faye. "Some men are very thrifty that way."

"The word is cheap," said Jenny. "I guess Gus came by to pick up the rest of his things and figured he'd stink up the place for old times' sake."

Faye grinned. "Sidney's been complaining the dry cleaner I use does terrible work. I haven't got the nerve to tell him I keep forgetting to send the stuff out."

Jenny looked up at the rows of bookshelves that lined the rear wall. It was one of the few home improvement projects that Gus had ever undertaken, and it was only after a year of nagging that he finally started. When he had actually begun working, he'd done a nice job. It seemed, now, a symbol of so

31

many things that had gone wrong. She should never have pushed him. The entire idea was really a sham anyway. The shelves were filled with books that friends were throwing away. The fact was that Gus never read anything, and Jenny, her pretentions to the contrary, was interested mainly in the women's magazines. "I never realized I had so many books," she said.

"Books expand the mind," said Faye. "Bagels expand the body. The trouble is, most books don't go well with cream cheese."

Jenny withdrew a thick paperback from a lower shelf. "Okay, *Gravity's Rainbow*, we'll try it one more time."

Faye followed Jenny into the bedroom, actually a partitioned-off corner. "You see," she said, "I think that's wrong."

"What? *Gravity's Rainbow*? I didn't even understand it."

"No, I mean to tackle heavyweight material at all. That is not what you should be doing now. I would read filth."

"When my divorce papers come, then I'll read filth. Until that time . . ."

"Try *The Heart's Silent Scream* by Viveca Cartwright. It's about a woman who discovers her husband has been raping young girls."

"I'll get to it," said Jenny. "But my present plans are to sit in a tub for a week with twelve pounds of junk food."

"Have room for a friend?"

"Sure."

Faye looked at her searchingly. "I feel so . . . helpless. Are you sure you'll be all right? Alone, I mean."

"After the last few years, I look forward to 'alone,'" said Jenny. "Now please go home."

Faye nodded. She crossed to the couch and picked up her coat, which had been slung over an armrest. "You must be exhausted."

Jenny nodded. "I just wanna crawl into bed and try to remember what my maiden name was."

"Will you call me?" said Faye, at the door.

"I will call you," said Jenny.

"Even if it's the middle of the night?"

"Even if it's the middle of the night."

"Sidney and I won't be doing anything," said Faye, "if that was one of your worries."

"It wasn't," said Jenny. "My worries are more convoluted. I could probably make the wife in *The Heart's Silent Scream* feel sorry for me."

Faye reached out to give her a quick hug.

"I love you, Faye."

Keeping her face averted so that Jenny wouldn't see the tears, Faye nodded and rushed out the door. Jenny listened to her footsteps on the stairs.

"Okay, folks," she said aloud, after a moment. "Let's take it one night at a time." She walked into the bedroom area, slipped out of her clothes, and put on a tattered old flannel nightgown. In the back of her mind were the words, *No one I have to impress now.* She felt a curious combination of freedom and melancholy. It must be something like this when your only child goes off to college, she thought. Not quite. That was natural, a maturing process, a growing away. What she had experienced was an abrupt severence. More like a Russian dissident suddenly exiled forever from the mother country. She lay down on the bed and opened *Gravity's*

Rainbow. The dissident image wasn't right either, she realized. Nothing seemed to be exactly analogous to being recently divorced. She began to read.

She was asleep before page five.

3

The ball seemed to linger in the sky, a spinning, hypnotic white sphere suspended against a background of electric blue. George, however, wasn't fooled. He'd spent too many years growing up on the crappy playing fields of the southeast Bronx. A studied athlete rather than a natural one, he backpedaled rapidly. That ball was not hanging, it was traveling. His experience told him to go back at least three feet behind where his eye-brain told him the ball would land. It came down in a lazy arc and George, running gracefully, made a neat, over-the-shoulder catch. Squeezing the ball in his glove, he reversed direction and headed toward the bench. It was the third out; now his team was due for its last turn at bat.

The games in Central Park were one of his purest pleasures. For two-and-a-half hours every Sunday, life was reduced to hitting, running, catching, and pitching. There were few subtleties or complexities, money was never involved, and an umpire solved all disputes. Too bad the rest of existence isn't like that, thought George, as he trotted alongside Leo, who played third base. Leo stopped most balls with his face.

"So finish the story," said Leo.

"What story?"

"You said it was ten-thirty and you were working on your book and the phone rings . . ."

"Oh, that," said George. "Yeah, that's right." They sat down on the bench. "It was ten-thirty, I'm working on my book, and the phone rang."

"That's it?"

The pitcher began taking his warm-ups. "It was a woman," said George. "Said her name was Leona Zorn."

"How'd she know you?"

"Oh, we met once. Her husband was my chiropractor. I stopped going to him after he wanted to cure my athlete's foot by spinal manipulation. Every other word out of his mouth was subluxation."

Leo opened a can of soda and drank half of it.

"Anyway," continued George, "she wanted to know if I'd like to have dinner Thursday night."

"The three of you?"

"Just her and me."

"Husband's out of town?"

"Well, in a way. He left her for a topless ice skater in Las Vegas."

Leo finished his soda and watched the first batter foul off the pitch. "What does she look like?"

"Like someone you'd leave for an ice skater in Las Vegas."

The batter cracked a sharp single to right field, faked heading for second, then returned to first base. "You're on deck, Big Schneider," called a stocky man at the end of the bench. George was called Big Schneider and Leo, Little Schneider, although Big Schneider was actually smaller than Little Schneider. George stood up and grabbed a couple of bats.

"So what's your problem?" said Leo.

"Women are calling me up for dates."

"That's it? What's your next gripe, somebody died and left you a lot of money?"

The new batter swung and missed.

"Four calls in two weeks," said George. "It never happened to me before. I was virtually a telephone virgin. I don't know how to handle it."

"Tell them to call me," said Leo. "I'll take care of them."

The batter swung and missed again.

"I mean, they're so open about everything," said George.

"That's the way people are nowadays," said Leo. "They think that letting all their disgusting, deviated perversions hang out makes them more likable."

"The first thing they do is tell you their status," said George. " 'How do you do, I've recently been widowed myself.' Or, 'Hi, I'm legally separated.' Or, 'Hello, I'm a divorcée.' "

"At least you know who you're dealing with."

"One woman called—swear to God!—I think her husband was just on vacation."

The batter hit a ground ball to the shortstop, who threw to the second baseman for a force play on the runner. George strode toward the cage.

"It's a competitive world, George," called Leo, posting himself behind the backstop to watch his brother bat. "The woman who sits waiting by the phone sits waiting by the phone."

37

"I got invited to three class reunions from schools I never went to," said George.

"Listen, if you're ready to move out amongst the living, George, let me take care of it, all right?"

"I don't think we live in the same worlds, Leo." George stepped into the batter's box.

"Trust me, Big Schneider. Just trust me."

"I'd trust you more if you stopped talking to me right now. Even Hank Aaron couldn't hit during a serious conversation."

The pitcher floated the ball toward the catcher. It was a slow-pitch league; the batter was permitted to choose and hit any ball he liked, a task more difficult than it looked. The pitches were lofted so high that by the time they descended toward home plate, they were traveling almost vertically. The swing had to be precisely timed and powerful, since almost all the momentum had to be supplied by the batter.

George let the first one go.

"Make him pitch to you, baby!" yelled Leo. "Make him pitch to you!"

Again, the pitcher delivered the ball. This time George lashed out, smashing a high line drive over shortstop. As he chugged toward first, he saw the ball bounce between the outfielders. Huffing and puffing, he strained toward second base. Heart attack, here I come, he thought. Tiny article on page 79 of the *News:* Writer Stricken in Broadway Show League. George Schneider, recently widowed author of several books, suffered a major coronary infarction . . . Gasping, red-faced, George rounded second base. He felt a numbness in his legs. There was a sense of detachment, as if his thighs were churning rapidly beneath him but were no longer connected to his torso. Three steps from third base, he went sprawling in the dirt. He made a few helpless crawling motions, heard the flat slap of the outfield relay as it hit the third baseman's glove, felt the tag against his shoulder.

Grinning sheepishly, he managed to get to his feet. He trotted in toward the bench, dusting off the seat of his trousers.

"You're out of shape, Georgie!" yelled Leo.

"At least the run scored," said George.

"Out of shape, kid," teased Leo.

George sat down on the bench. "Out of shape, my ass."

"Especially that," said Leo.

• • • •

The name of the place was Le Coq D'Or, and the ladies' room was marked *Mesdames.* Inside, Jenny looked in the mirror and carefully freshened her lipstick. It had not been a good evening. The food had been mediocre, the prices high, the service haughty, and her date . . . not for her. She ran a comb through her hair and started for the door. The attendant handed her a towel.

"Uh, that's all right, I didn't use the sink," said Jenny.

"Take it anyway," said the woman, "you may need it."

Jenny hesitated. She knew if she accepted the towel she'd have to give the woman a tip, which she did not believe in. It was a matter of principle. "I really don't want it," she said.

"It's free," said the woman. "A souvenir."

Jenny shook her head and crossed toward the door. "You'll be sorry," called the woman. "One day you'll think about this, and you'll be paralyzed with guilt."

Jenny made her way through the restaurant to her table.

"Everything okay?" said the man waiting for her. His name was Gary.

"Fine," said Jenny. Thoughts flew through her head. A month from now, thumbing through a newspaper, she would see an article about the ladies' room attendant at the Coq D'Or, dead of malnutrition. The customers simply stopped tipping, a saddened manager would tell reporters.

"Ready?" said Gary.

"Yes," said Jenny.

He stood up. This was a major event because he was six-feet-eleven-inches tall. "And don't know which end of a basketball is up," he had told Jenny. She noticed other patrons trying to hide their stares.

"I just called Regine's, if that's all right with you," Gary said.

"You mean dancing?" asked Jenny.

"Well, we could stand outside and have the bouncer heap abuse on us," said Gary.

Jenny smiled thinly. The thought of dancing with someone a foot and a half taller than she was did not hold great attraction. Her face reflected her feelings.

"We don't have to go if you don't want to," said Gary.

"No, no, I'm sure we'll have lots of fun," lied Jenny. Even with men of normal height, she'd always been a lousy dancer. (She'd taken hustle lessons on two separate occasions, each time without Gus, and forgotten the steps almost as quickly as she learned them. "Easy come, easy go," she'd told friends.)

Heads turned as Gary and Jenny proceeded toward the exit. In the lobby, Jenny said, "One second," and crossed to the ladies' room. Inside, she handed fifty cents to the attendant, who eyed it disdainfully, and stuffed it back into Jenny's palm.

"I happen to be an heiress," said the woman, and Jenny fled.

Outside, flustered, Jenny scarcely noticed the middle-aged man and bizarrely coiffed girl who brushed right by her. She waited uncertainly, pacing back and forth in a tight pattern, while her eighty-three-inch date struggled to hail a cab.

•   •   •   •

In the restaurant, the same heads that had swiveled at the passage of the giant now swiveled back to follow the young lady in a skintight sequined dress and black hair with the red-and-white center stripe. The maitre d', as if unwilling to accept this apparition, addressed himself only to her escort.

"Monsieur? Can I help you?"

"Yes," said the man uncomfortably. "At least in one respect, maybe. I have a reservation."

"Name?"

"Schneider."

"*Pardon?*"

The man cleared his throat, but kept his voice very low. "George Schneider."

The maitre d' consulted his book.

"I called late," said George. "If you don't have it, I understand."

"I have been here twenty-two years," said the maitre d', "and never have I lost a reservation."

"Hear that, Bambi," said George to the girl. "Man's been here twenty-two years."

Bambi found this amusing. She gave an irregular, choking laugh that sounded like a chicken being abused under water. George wished he were in Thailand.

"Yes!" said the maitre d' suddenly. "Here we are. Schneider. Party of two."

"Something in the back would be nice," said George softly. "Far in the back."

"Certainly," said the matire d'.

"More privacy," explained George to Bambi.

"If you'll follow me," said the maitre d', heading for a table near the kitchen, a table that was set aside for just such a circumstance.

● ● ● ●

A few days later, Jenny and Faye stood in the lobby of the Public Theater and tried to figure out the Joe Papp production they were seeing. It was first act intermission, and the people were packed shoulder to shoulder.

"Did you get the part where he bites the heads off the sardines?" asked Jenny. "I had the feeling that was important, but I couldn't quite understand it."

"I assumed it was symbolic," said Faye. "I guess that was the way he's supposed to have treated his wife."

Jenny shrugged. "I love Colleen, but so far I honestly don't know what the hell this play's about."

"Don't worry," said Faye, "you're in good company. John Simon wrote that he couldn't understand this play either."

"But he didn't understand it on a higher level," said Jenny.

"Never mind," said Faye. "Simon said they ought to follow the author around with a pooper scooper. So much for higher levels."

"I also don't see why the wife smeared Crisco on his *Scientific American* collection. That was supposed to be very dramatic, but I didn't get it."

"Maybe they'll explain it to you in Cleveland," said Faye.

"All right," said Jenny. "I know how you feel about my hometown."

"I like Cleveland," protested Faye. "It makes Philadelphia look lively."

"All right. . . ."

"I hear they even have a movie theater there now."

"Listen," said Jenny, "Cleveland has a population of eight hundred thousand, and—"

"That's one apartment building in Bensonhurst," said Faye.

Jenny smiled; she'd heard the routine before. "I know, I know. Any day now the mayor is expected to reach puberty. All right, pick on someplace else for a change."

Faye shrugged. "How long will you be there?"

"Just a few days," said Jenny. "I woke up one

43

morning with an overwhelming desire to sleep in the bed I was born in."

Faye nodded soberly. "It's my fault, isn't it?"

"What?"

"Was the other night really terrible?"

Jenny inhaled deeply. "I accepted the date. I didn't expect any miracles."

"Oh, come on!" snapped Faye. "You don't have to be polite with me. It's not like you bought my car, or something."

"Well . . ." said Jenny. "It's just . . . I didn't expect anyone six-foot-eleven-inches tall. I mean, when we were standing up I found myself face to face with his fly. It was a little disconcerting."

"He didn't get fresh, did he?"

"Oh, no, no. Not at all. He was very nice and polite. Formal, even. Maybe too formal. The trouble was me. My fault entirely. I've always been afraid of heights."

"Sidney told me he was a big man from Chicago," said Faye. "I didn't think he meant literally."

"I couldn't stop wondering," said Jenny, "about, you know, in bed . . ."

"Oh, those things work out somehow," said Faye. "The human body is very flexible, and the human mind very ingenious."

"When so motivated."

"Of course."

"And the other thing I kept thinking of," said Jenny, "was what if we got married and I had a baby? I'd be giving birth for days."

Faye giggled, then abruptly turned away. "Hide me," she whispered urgently.

"What?"

"There's someone over there I don't want to see."

"Where?"

"Don't ask where, just put me inside your coat."

Across the lobby, the someone Faye Medwick didn't want to see was talking expansively to two distinguished looking men. "Joe's very excited about this one," he said. "Thinks we got a hell of a shot." His eyes continuously scanned the lobby. "Listen," he said to the men, "I'll catch you backstage after the show, we'll talk. Nice seeing you." He pushed his way through the crowd.

"Oh, God!" said Faye. "He's coming over."

"Who?" said Jenny.

"Leo Schneider. Shit, my luck."

"Who's Leo Schneider?"

"A press agent. I dated him years ago, before I met Sidney."

"You mean back at the dawn of history...."

"Yes. You know. Before Man became erect. Or at least before Leo did. Anyway, he used to call me Faysie. That's what broke us up."

Leo now stood three feet away, eyes open wide, arms spread. "Faysie!"

"Who?" said Faye.

"I can't believe it. You look absolutely fabulous. How are you?" Leo hugged Faye ostentatiously, his standard publicity-agent embrace.

"Hello, Leo," said Faye. She turned toward Jenny. "Leo Schneider, Jenny MacLaine."

"Hello," said Jenny.

Leo nodded and smiled. "Hi. Nice to meet

45

you." He extended a hand, which Jenny shook, and stared at her rudely. "Why do you look familiar?"

"I don't know," said Jenny. "Did you go to P.S. Seventy-nine in Cleveland?"

"I make it a point never to even *fly* over Cleveland," said Leo.

Jenny shrugged. "Then it beats me. Faye, why do I look familiar?"

"Should I tell him?" said Faye.

"Up to you," said Jenny.

"What's going on?" said Leo.

"We did a soap opera a few years ago," explained Faye. "Jenny is still a little sheepish about it, but a lot of people saw it, and occasionally there were some well written scenes."

"What was the name?" asked Leo.

"*The World Rotates*," said Faye. "We shot it in a Brooklyn studio for Proctor and Gamble, three days a week, twelve-hour days."

"I guess I must've passed near a set when you were on," said Leo to Jenny.

"She's the best damn actress in New York," said Faye fiercely. "You ought to tell your friend Joe Papp about her."

"Sure," said Leo, still facing Jenny. "Why don't you give me a call in the office?"

"You think there's any chance—"

"We're doing five new plays this year," said Leo. "All you stand to lose is a dime. Call."

"Thank you," said Jenny. "I will. I'm always interested in good work." Suddenly she felt a rush of blood to her face. In one more minute, she thought, I'll break out in a sweat. "I have to get some air, Faye," she said. "Nice meeting you, Mr. Schneider."

"Same here," said Leo, watching as Jenny pushed her way through the crowd. "Nice meeting me," he added. He returned his attention to Faye. "Interesting looking girl. . . ."

"Interesting to whom?" said Faye.

Leo grinned. "Years ago you would've said 'to who,' Faysie. You've advanced in the world."

"And you still evade questions."

"You're right," said Leo briskly. "Interesting to me."

"You're not married anymore?"

"I am."

"But you cheat." A half question.

Leo smiled. "You see how quickly a potential good deed can be misinterpreted. I happen to have a brother who recently lost his wife. You remember my brother?"

Faye thought back. "Not real—Wait a minute. Yeah, yeah. Didn't we go bowling together once, a double date?"

"Sounds right."

"He kept complaining he couldn't find a ball?"

"That would be standard for George."

"I think I remember him."

"So," said Leo, "is Jenny, uh—"

"Available?"

"Yeah."

"Maybe."

"You'll tell me a little about her?"

"Maybe."

Leo grinned. "Jesus, you look incredible, Faysie." He looked around. "Where's Sidney?"

"In Indianapolis on business," said Faye. "Where's Marilyn?"

47

"In Indianapolis on business." Leo inhaled theatrically. "Is that the same perfume I gave you seven years ago?"

"You expected me to save it?"

Leo regarded her carefully, a nonprofessional gaze this time. "No," he said quietly. "I guess not."

Faye hesitated. "Well, I did anyway," she said. A lie, of course. Why, she wondered, did she feel compelled to dramatize? "Although, naturally, this isn't it."

Leo nodded. "So," he said after a moment. "Fill me in on your life, before the end of intermission."

The crowd had largely disappeared back into the theater by the time Faye found Jenny leaning against a wall near the box office. She was sipping a Coke from a small cup.

"Eighty-five cents they charge for this," said Jenny. "Can you believe it?"

"Second act's starting," said Faye. "We better get back."

Jenny nodded and held out the cup. "Want a quarter's worth?" she said, eyeing the half inch of soda remaining.

Faye shook her head. "You should've hung around. Joe Papp came by. Leo wanted to introduce you."

"I'm sorry," said Jenny. "I just couldn't breathe in there. I really have to get out of New York for a while."

The second-act buzzer sounded. "Well, don't stay too long," said Faye. "You're going to get a call this week."

Jenny felt a thrill of excitement. "From Joe Papp?"

"From George Schneider."

"You mean that guy we met? Faye—"

"That was Leo. George is his brother."

Jenny rolled her eyes toward the ceiling. "Faye, you promised . . ." She drained her cup, flipped it in a garbage pail, and headed for the next act.

"He's a writer," said Faye, trailing her.

"I am not in the meat market," said Jenny.

"And he's not shopping." Faye was having a hard time catching up to Jenny on the stairs. "I met him once. Not gorgeous, but sweet looking, with an intelligent face. His wife died about six months ago."

Jenny paused at the top of the stairs. "Well, *I* didn't," she said, "and I'm not interested in a replacement part." She headed for their seats. "This play is depressing enough," she added.

•   •   •   •

The house was in the Ludlow section of Shaker Heights, an integrated neighborhood. Thirty years earlier, when Jenny was growing up, the area had been all white, but gradually the blacks moved in, and the original residents fled. But Jenny's parents had held their ground.

"I got nothin' against Negroes," Jenny's father had said. "I work with 'em all day, don't see why I got to run away from 'em at night. Besides, nobody's gonna push me outa my own house."

Jenny's mother would have preferred flight, but there was little she could do. She was one of those

49

weak, sheltered women who deferred to their husbands in all major decisions and kept their resentments to themselves. Jenny's father, a tool-and-die maker, was fortunately not a tyrant, but neither did he believe in household democracy. "I run a tight ship," he would tell friends and co-workers proudly. Carolyn, Jenny's older sister, was properly fearful and impressed. Jenny wasn't.

The walls of Jenny's room were covered with yellowing wallpaper, a mundane print pattern that had seemed to begin its fade immediately after delivery. Shafts of sunlight filtered through dusty blinds; regardless of season, there was always a sense of summer ennui, a melancholy, paralyzing timelessness. Jenny's life was illustrated by photographs on the wall, the older black-and-whites augmented by the artificial coloring popular long ago. Jenny at three, sitting on a swing in some long-gone park. Carolyn and Jenny together, arms around each other, Jenny age six. Jenny at twelve, her wrist in a cast. Twelve had been a bad year. She'd begun menstruating unexpectedly in the middle of class, endured a hasty, embarrassing exit, refused to return for a week. A month later she'd had an emergency appendectomy; no sooner had she recovered than she broke her wrist in a freak fall from her bicycle, which her father thereafter refused to let her ride. Somehow, she'd become a teenager. Jenny at sixteen, a supporting role in her high school play, the first time she'd shown any enthusiasm for any scholastic activity.

"It's not a sensible plan," her father said, when she announced she wanted to major in drama at college. "Do you know how few women actually make it to the stage? Or the screen? There's no percentage in it, it'll only bring you heartache."

"It's that or nothing," said Jenny.

"Then it's nothing," her father announced. "I'm not paying two thousand a year so my daughter can waste her time."

He'd changed his mind. Jenny had enrolled at Northwestern, gotten a night job as a salesgirl to pay the tuition. After the first year, the tool-and-die maker relented. "To me, it seems a waste of good potential," he admitted, "but seein' as you're so serious about it . . ."

Jenny at nineteen, framed in gold, Lady Mac-Beth in her sophomore class play. Jenny at twenty, bridesmaid at Carolyn's wedding to an insurance salesman. Jenny at graduation, she radiant, her parents unable to conceal their glumness. She'd just announced her intention to go to New York. "It's not a sensible plan," her father had said. This time her mother agreed. Jenny at twenty-four, a different kind of photograph, this one sleekly professional, posed, a proof from a model's portfolio. Newspaper articles: Jenny in a bit part in *Li'l Abner*. Jenny filling in, in *The Fantasticks*. Jenny in an Ipana commercial. Jenny in a soap opera. (*"Our Jenny? On television?"*) It was not shown in Cleveland.

Jenny glanced anxiously at the clock. Ten minutes to eleven. Nighttime. A chancy hour to call. She finished dialing and lay back against the headboard.

"Faye?" she said.

"Who. . . . Jenny?"

"Did I wake you?"

"No, no, not at all. I gave up sleep about six

51

months ago. I noticed it was taking up too much of my time. Anyway, how are you? How's metropolis? You still planning to come back Saturday?"

"I'm fine," said Jenny. "Right this second I'm lying in the bed I was born in."

"No kidding? You must be enjoying yourself."

"I'm coming back Wednesday, Faye, not Saturday."

"You're not enjoying yourself."

"It's a funny thing," said Jenny. "I wanted to go back to some kind of an anchor, some kind of island where everything was stable. It's what you do, I guess, when you feel your life becoming rootless, when everything seems to be shifting under you." She paused. In the next room, she could hear her father snoring. He'd be sleeping in an undershirt and shorts, as he always did, and her mother would be reading a paperback. "The trouble is," she continued, "I can't stand the very quality I wanted to find. Everything here is the same. Nothing changes. I think the difference between stability and stagnation is whether you live there or not."

Faye waited a moment before speaking. "My best psychological evaluation is that you're all fucked up," she said. "And if that's the way you're gonna think, you may as well do it in New York. At least here you'll be with the majority."

Jenny shook her head. "I found out that the only thing more depressing than my future is my past," she said.

From the last picture on the wall, she seemed to look down on herself, a frozen confirmation of her judgment preserved on an eight-by-ten glossy: Jenny and Gus on the day of their wedding.

4

George's fingers flew over the typewriter. At least in his imagination, that is. Actually, they sort of walked over the typewriter, tripped occasionally, crawled when he became tired. Typing was not one of his strongpoints; twenty words a minute was close to his top speed. Fortunately, he was a slow thinker too, and so did not have to face the problem of running ahead of himself. He was, however, a *professional* writer and knew the professional's secret: Slow and steady wins the race. Or, at least, keeps you *in* the race. A thousand words a day was a novel four months later. Counting time spent on revisions, he could produce two book-length manuscripts a year, enough to keep him alive. The problem, as always, was the thousand daily words. So simple, yet so difficult. A totally unreasonable process. There were days when he felt quite wonderful, alert, energetic—and for some reason could not write two readable sentences. Other times, sulky, depressed, expecting to quit after a few halfhearted minutes, he'd find the prose pouring out, effortless, fluid, as if some literary artery had been opened in his brain.

Today's output had fallen, as was most often the case, somewhere between the extremes. Rushes of three or four paragraphs were followed by thirty minutes of numbed stasis. He'd ignored several phone calls. At 4:30 P.M. there was a knock on the door. "Yeah?" said George, as he opened it.

It was Leo in his softball outfit, carrying an Adidas bag, streaked with mud. "We got creamed," he said, barging in.

"What score?" said George, shutting the door.

"Seventeen to two. We made eight errors. Where the hell were you?"

"Did you wipe your feet?"

"What?"

"Your feet, your feet. You're leaving footprints like a yeti all over the carpet."

"So you'll vacuum," said Leo, heading for the kitchen.

"I just *had* the place cleaned," protested George.

Leo opened the refrigerator. "It's only dirt," he said. "Don't get excited. Pure, clean Central Park dirt. It'll dry right up." He took out a can of beer.

"How can dirt be clean?" asked George.

"You still haven't told me what's been happening to you lately. You don't pick up your phone for four days?"

"I've been busy."

"You don't return your messages."

"I've been *cleaning up* the apartment."

"For four days?"

"I haven't been feeling too great, Leo." George leaned into the refrigerator, took out a container of milk, and poured himself half a glass.

54

"You got yellow fever?" asked Leo. "Scurvy? Beriberi?"

George took some Mallomars from a box in the cupboard. "I've been writing. I wrote three hundred pages of my new book."

"So you weren't sick."

"I was. I haven't thought of a story yet." He followed Leo back into the living room.

"You should call, you know," said Leo.

"I know."

"I worry about you."

"I know. I'm sorry." George bit into one of the Mallomars.

"Listen," said Leo, "I just need two minutes of your time because we have serious business to discuss."

George stood at his desk, leafing through some papers. "Wait a minute. Before the serious business. What's the name of that researcher you told me about? The old lady who works at the Columbia Library?"

"You need it right now?"

"I have to have that book on Edwin Booth. I can't find it." Edwin Booth was the model for one of the characters in his novel, a successful but unhappy actor. George's work energy had begun to flag when he'd read about Booth's first marriage to a wife who died very young.

Leo pulled a tiny piece of paper from his wallet. "Jurgens," he said. "Serena Jurgens." He tossed the paper on George's desk. "George, you gotta listen to me, I think I found buried treasure."

"I'm not diving anymore, Leo."

"This is the real goods, George."

"Your last week's goods gave me the bends. Jenkins, did you say, or Jurgens?"

"Jurgens. I apologize, okay?"

"Accepted."

"You didn't like Bambi, what can I tell you."

George dialed the number Leo had given him, waited, got a busy signal. He hung up. "Where do you find them, Leo? Did you ever actually meet her?"

"Sure I met her."

"With the red and white zigzag streak in her hair?"

"When I saw it, it was blond . . . and straight. Lots of people have blond streaks."

"She looked like the cover of a record album, Leo. Like her beautician had a seizure."

Leo wiped some Budweiser foam from his lips. He grinned. "But a terrific body. You gotta admit that body was put together by someone very close to God."

George began packing batches of papers into a leather portfolio. "I booked a table in one of the best French restaurants in New York. And there I am in my blue suit with this creature from *Star Wars*."

Leo shrugged. "I told you not to go anyplace fancy. You take her to New Jersey."

"Like where? A diner, maybe?"

"Yeah. . . ."

"Don't be ridiculous." George zipped the portfolio closed. "You know what kind of dress she was wearing? Electric. I swear to God, we got in and the cab driver got static on his radio."

"But you had a good time, right? I went to a lot of trouble, George."

"I'd hate to think what would've happened if things had come easy for you." George licked the last bit of Mallomar from his fingers.

"At least tell me you had a good time," persisted Leo.

"I did not."

"You did. You just can't admit it."

George shook his head. "What do you mean, 'a good time'? A thunderstorm came up. I'm sitting there with a lightning rod." He put on a jacket that had been draped over a closet doorknob. "I did not have a good time. She ordered a nine dollar goose liver plate and made a hero sandwich out of it. Leave me alone, Leo." He tried dialing the number again, but it was still busy.

"George, I have set that girl up with some very heavy clients from Hollywood—"

"What?"

"I said—"

"What are you telling me?"

"—and they've been very nice to me every Christmas."

"Are you telling me she's a hooker?" George clapped a hand to his forehead. "Are you saying that outlet from Con Edison is a pro?"

Leo shook his head. "Would I do that to you? My brother?"

"Who knows? Who understands what goes through that head of yours?"

Leo held out his palms. "Relax, please. Save the hysteria for when you need it. She's a terrific kid, Bambi. A little flashy, yes—"

"Like a welding torch."

"A little Art Deco with the wardrobe, yes. But no hooker." Leo paused uncertainly. "Why, did she charge you anything?"

George collected his keys and some loose change from the top of his desk. "For what? I have a low threshold for electrocution, I was afraid to touch her."

Leo placed his beer can on the floor, walked to the desk, and picked up the paper that he'd used for the researcher's phone number. He scribbled something on the other side. "I have a feeling about this new one, George."

"Lie down until it passes."

"This is really Class A material."

"I am not a beef inspector."

"All you have to do is call her. I wrote the number for you."

George squinted at his brother. "Leo . . . please. I have my work, I have my friends, I have my family. I have the Knicks, the Jets, the Rangers, the Yankees, the Giants and the Mets. This season is taken care of. So is next season. And the one after that."

"George, I'm not talking sports now. Man cannot live by sports alone. Although I admit he can come close."

"I understand," said George. "Believe me, I appreciate. But you have to understand also. I don't expect to find another Barbara, that's never going to happen."

"George, you—"

"But I *will* go out. I *will* meet people. But I have to find them in my own time, in my own way. I love you for what you're doing . . . but don't do it

58

anymore." George stuffed the sheet of scratch paper in his jacket pocket and headed for the front door.

His tone would have intimidated most people, but Leo was unaffected. Younger brothers adjust at an early age to attempted bullying by older siblings. "Where are you going?" he asked.

"To work in privacy," said George. "If you follow me, I'll break your legs."

Leo followed him into the hall. "So don't call her! What do I care?"

George stalked toward the elevator, leaving his brother to lock the door.

"Live your life like a monk," continued Leo. "Stay in here and make brandy. It's not my business. You want to be a hermit? An outcast? You want to be antisocial? Go ahead. It's a free country . . ."

And so it went, down six floors and out into the street.

•   •   •   •

George sat at a table in the first floor reading room of the New York Public Library. Papers and books were scattered around him, and he made notes on a small pad. After a while he stretched, then yawned. He glanced at his watch. 7:00 P.M.; he'd been there two hours. He stood up and moved a short distance away from the table. A black teen-ager approached him. " 'Scuse me."

"You want me?"

"Yeah. Could you page mah frien'?"

"I don't think paging is permitted," said George.

"His name's Boo. He ain' all there, see. Sometime, he git lost."

"I don't think I can help you," said George.

"You work here?"

"No."

"You don't work here?"

"No."

The teenager, a tall, spindly boy with hair in tight black ringlets, seemed puzzled. "How come you don't?"

"I just don't," said George. "I'm sorry."

The teenager nodded. "Hey, maybe Boo is takin' a shit, you think so?"

"I wouldn't know. It's possible."

"Where the men's room here?"

"Third floor," said George. "You go out the door, turn right, and you'll come to the elevators. Bathroom is on the third floor."

"You okay, man," said the boy, walking off.

Some people are easily satisfied, George thought. He gathered up his things, slipped on his jacket, and started out into the corridor. Halfway to the exit turnstiles, he spotted a bank of public phones. He squeezed into a booth, closed the door, and extracted from his pocket the slip of notepaper Leo had given him. He inserted a dime into the phone, dialed, and waited through five rings. Just as he was about to hang up, a breathless female voice answered.

"Hello?"

Jenny was gasping. She'd heard the phone from the corridor, had run through the hall with her heavy suitcase. It was not a rational thing to do, but it was irresistible. Who could endure a ringing phone without finding out who it was? She now fought for oxygen.

George squinted at the notepaper. "Hello? Is

this, uh . . . I'm sorry, I'm not sure I have your name right."

"Hello?" said Jenny, more as a sign of impatience than a greeting. It was a salesman, she thought, some yo-yo who wanted her to buy mutual funds or life insurance.

"This is George Schneider," said George. "Leo Schneider's brother?"

"Who?"

"I believe he told you I'd be calling."

"I'm sorry, I don't have any funds to invest right now, Mr. Schneider."

"No, no," said George, "you must have me confused. I'm George Schneider."

"I'm supposed to know you?"

"I'm a writer."

Jenny sat down on the suitcase. "Oh . . . God, yes." It was coming back. "George Schneider. My friend Faye mentioned something, but . . . it seemed so long ago."

Who the hell was Faye? George wondered. A fan perhaps? One of the eighteen people in the world who'd read his books?

"I'm sorry," continued Jenny. "You caught me at a bad time. I just got off a plane and walked in the door. Ran in the door, actually." And I have to pee like crazy, she added mentally.

"I see," said George. "Maybe I should call you back."

"Well . . ." said Jenny. "Look, I'll be very honest with you, Mr. Schneider. I'm going through a transition period right now. The truth is, I'm not really planning to date for quite a while."

"Date?"

"Yes. . . ."

"Did Leo say I was going to call you for a date?"

Jenny was too tired to feel embarrassed. "Well, he said you were going to call, so I assumed—"

"No, no," said George, amazed that an octogenarian was still interested in pursuing an active social life. It should happen to me, he thought. "This wasn't a date call," he explained. "My brother is a bit of a prankster, see. Actually, I'm very surprised at Leo, Miss, uh . . . is it Jenkins or Jurgens?"

"Is what?"

"Your name?"

"It's MacLaine. Jennifer MacLaine."

George peered steadily at the paper. "Jennifer MacLaine?" He shook his head. "No. That's wrong."

"I could show you my driver's license."

"That's not the name he gave me . . ."

"But it's *my* name, Mr. Schneider. I turn around when people call me by it."

With a flash of insight, George flipped the paper over. "Oh, Jesus!" he moaned. "You're the one on the other side."

"Depends where you're standing," said Jenny. "Are we finished now?"

"Your name was on the back of a note my brother left," explained George. "I couldn't read his writing. His penmanship looks like what other people spill. Serena Jurgens was the one I wanted."

"I'm not Serena Jurgens."

"I understand that now. She's a librarian, about eighty-five years old."

"Well, you know what you want better than I do."

"This is very embarrassing."

"I promise not to tell if you won't," said Jenny. Nature's call was becoming a shout. "Shall we say good-bye, then?"

"I really was going to call you socially," said George. "At another time. I really was."

"Good," said Jenny. "Let's see how it goes with Serena first, okay? Good-bye." She hung up, shook her head in amazement, and raced for the bathroom.

In the phone booth, George was muttering. "Goddammit, Leo, get your women straight, will-ya!" He stuffed the piece of paper back into his pocket, opened the door, and left the library. On impulse, he decided to walk through Bryant Park. As a child, he had often been taken there by his father; the two of them would sit on a bench and feed the pigeons. Sometimes, a pigeon would fly up to perch on his shoulder and try to nibble directly from his little bag of Planter's Peanuts. "They like the salt," his father would say as George squealed in delight.

"Wanna score some coke?" said a man coming toward him.

"No thanks," said George. The man was dressed in a shabby overcoat. A livid scar ran the length of his face.

"What you want, then?"

George took a step sideways. "I'm sorry," he said.

The man moved to block his path. "Hey, man, I got everything. Uppers, downers, poppers, snappers, scag . . . just tell me which one you after."

George looked around. It was dusk. There were

only a few people scattered in the park—as if they would help!—no cops. He prepared himself to be stabbed. "I'm really not into drugs," he said.

"It's a good deal," said the man. "You should try it. Gimme a ten, an' I'll let you have some bargains." He took another step in George's direction.

Suddenly, a very large black man came up behind them. George had a quick image: himself prostrate from a million different knife wounds, pigeons drinking from the tiny pools of blood that peppered the walk. *They like the salt.* "This guy botherin' you?" asked the black man. He wore a vest and cabdriver cap.

"Well ..." said George.

"Fuck off," said the man to the pusher, "or your face be lookin' out the other side your head."

The pusher retreated. "Okay, okay. No sweat. Jus' makin' a introductory offer." He disappeared through an opening in a thick clump of bushes.

The teenager whom George had directed in the library peeked around from behind the black man, smiling toothily. "This here is Boo," he said, indicating his giant friend. "Looked like you was gittin' hassled."

George exhaled. "Thanks," he said. "I appreciate your intervention."

"I didn' invent nothin'," said the boy.

"And thank you, Boo," said George.

The man said nothing.

George glanced at his watch, as if he were late for some appointment. "I gotta go," he said. "Thanks again."

"See you tomorrow," said the boy.

George walked rapidly out of the park. His

heart was thumping crazily inside the paper chamber of his chest. He definitely would not be there tomorrow. Introductory dope offers and easily lost people named Boo were not the sort of lures he found enticing. He crossed Forty-second street, located a luncheonette, and sat down in a booth. The place was still fairly crowded with late-working businessmen and tourists. George ordered a hamburger, french fries and coffee. After a half hour, he managed to relax. On the way out, he spotted a public phone near the cashier. He dialed, and let it ring.

"Hello?"

"It's me," said George. "I'm back."

Jenny was not thrilled to hear this. She was dressed in a towel, having been just about to step into a steaming bath. Steaming baths were one of life's greatest pleasures. "You and the old lady didn't hit it off?" she asked.

"*Now* I know who you are," said George. "I was almost killed and my life flashed in front of me, and suddenly I remembered."

"You realized who I was when you were almost killed?"

"Well, I wasn't *just* almost killed," said George. "It was about forty minutes ago. But the point is, I have it straight now. Leo told me about you, I was on the way out."

"You mean, as you were dying your brother brought me up?" Jenny wondered if George was drunk.

"No, no. As I was leaving the apartment, Leo wrote your name down on a scrap of paper."

"Who could ask for more than that?" said Jenny.

Behind George, a waitress dropped a stack of

plates. The luncheonette crowd cheered as he pressed his ear to the receiver. "I'm calling back," he explained, "because I wanted you to know that I got the numbers mixed up, and I didn't want you to think I wasn't calling you. I was. I mean, I wasn't *then*. I am *now*."

"That's good," said Jenny. "For a minute I thought I might be dreaming this. I guess not. Okay, so now you're calling me. For a date?"

"No."

"Not a date. To sell me something?"

"No."

"I'm not a librarian, so if it's not for a date, then what exactly—"

"It's not for a date *yet*. I mean, I thought I'd wait and explain the *last* call before I went ahead with the next one."

Jenny felt her towel slipping. The living room window shades were not drawn. The voyeurs would be in heaven. "I'm a little slow," she said. "Which call are we on now?"

"This is the call back to explain the dumb call. The charming call comes after we hang up from this one." There was a metallic click, and then an operator's voice interrupted. "Time's up. Signal when through."

"—got this message on—"

"Excuse me?" said George.

"I said," repeated Jenny, "if I got this message on my answering service, I'd need a private detective."

"I'll tell you the absolute truth," said George. "I haven't made a call to a nice girl in fourteen years. I wasn't even good at it then. If I seem inept, please bear with me."

"You seem ept enough," said Jenny. "The point is, Mr... uh...."

"Schneider."

"The point is, Mr. Schneider, as I told Faye to tell Leo to tell you ... I may be leaving town next week."

"I see...." Brush-off, thought George.

"I may be going to Washington to do some repertory work, and this is a bad time to ... well, to meet anyone." The steaming bath would no longer be steaming, Jenny knew. She would have to refill the tub.

"Sure," said George. "I understand."

"Nice speaking to you," said Jenny brusquely. "Good-bye." She hung up.

George stood there a moment, then headed out of the luncheonette. He heard the phone ring as he went through the door. He knew the call was for him—he owed money—and yet, for some reason, he just kept going. He was annoyed, annoyed in general. He wasn't going to pay. Other people never did, why should he? Enough of being the patsy. He walked briskly toward Sixth Avenue, then heard a man shouting behind him. "Hey! Hey, you!"

He turned. It was the owner of the luncheonette, white apron around his waist, running after him, gesturing. George fled west along Forty-second. In a moment, he knew, the man would stop a cop and point in George's direction. The officer, gun drawn, would peg three quick shots into George's spine, leaving him crippled, reducing his typing speed even below what it was now. George ducked into a movie theater, slid two dollars through the box office cage, and hurried into the interior darkness.

About halfway down one of the aisles, he stood

still a moment to let his eyes adjust to the lack of light. On-screen was a close-up of somebody's vagina, enlarged perhaps fifty times. Now the gargantuan head of a penis came into view. At these magnifications, the effect was dizzying rather than erotic, remote, detached from the act being depicted. It looked like a battle of marine monsters. A giant mushroom from the deep was attacking an outsized mollusk.

George retreated up the aisle into the lobby. There he found a phone, went to it, dialed, and waited. "Hi! This is the charming call," he said.

"I think I have a problem on my hands," said Jenny. She was in the midst of unpacking.

"You don't," said George. "I promise. This is definitely our last conversation."

"Then why did you call back?"

"I couldn't resist saying, 'This is the charming call.' "

"It's your dime," said Jenny.

"Seriously," said George, "I realize I'm intruding on your privacy. I know how you feel. But I liked the sound of your voice and the way you handled yourself."

And now comes the pitch, thought Jenny.

"So," continued George, "I just wanted to say, 'Good luck with your repertory and the rest of your life, and this is now the end of the charming call.' Good-bye." He hung up, feeling massively satisfied.

Jenny, puzzled, felt faintly disappointed.

George moved toward the theater exit. He wondered if the luncheonette owner might still be waiting for him, accompanied now by four squad cars of heavily armed police. George would step outside, a bullhorn would bark an incomprehensible order,

and as he hesitated in the glaring spotlights, a fusil-
lade of bullets would cut him down. Better that
than watching the giant sea monsters, thought
George. He strolled out into the night.

5

On the way home, he picked up a takeout order of Chinese food. Hot-and-sour soup. Shredded beef with garlic sauce. Sweet-and-sour duck with lichee nuts, cherries, and mandarin oranges. Feeling somehow like a criminal, he carried this delightful booty up to his apartment and attacked it as soon as he'd closed the door. It was absolutely sinful, he thought, stuffing down great hunks of the pungent, aromatic treasure. Let the guy in Bryant Park have his angel dust and Quaaludes—the true highs in life could be found at *Ting Wa* (Plus, they threw in fortune cookies.).

George finished the beef dish first, then tore into the still-hot duck. Gradually, he began to eat more slowly, the killer pangs of Szechuan lust beginning to fade. He hadn't told them to leave out the MSG; in a half hour, he knew, he'd be close to paralysis. He staggered over to his jacket, fished out the piece of notepaper, made his way to the phone. The fact was that he felt like talking to someone, even if only to share his appreciation of the Chinese food.

"Hello?"

"Hi," said George. "Me again."

Jenny, too, happened to be eating. A salad made with crisp, fresh lettuce, tomatoes, scallions, cucumbers, and green peppers. Diet Italian dressing. A cup of tea. She had been turning the pages of *Catch-22; Gravity's Rainbow* had proved too tough. Again, she was not delighted with the phone call. "George Schneider?" she said.

"I was trying all day to place your voice," said George.

"And you'll keep calling till you do, is that it?"

"California girl, right? U.C.L.A.?"

"My God!" said Jenny.

George chuckled smugly. "A writer learns to develop an ear for these things, if he doesn't have it already, that is."

"I was born in Cleveland," said Jenny.

"You were?" No smugness now.

"And I went to Bennington, in Vermont."

"Well," said George, chuckling sheepishly. "How about that? I was so close."

"Matter of fact, that's where I've just come from," said Jenny.

"Bennington?"

"Cleveland. I was visiting family."

"Aha," said George.

"Aha what?"

"Just aha. Acknowledgment. Comprehension. I understand."

"Oh. Well, aha to you too."

George smiled. "You know, Leo really did say you were something special. I just didn't pay attention." He popped a lichee nut into his mouth and covered the receiver while he chewed. The flavor seemed to penetrate directly into his brain.

"Why didn't you pay attention?" asked Jenny.

"Past history."

"What?"

"His previous social arrangements for me all ended like the Andrea Doria."

"And yet here you are calling me," said Jenny.

"Only by mistake."

"No, no. The first call was a mistake. The second wasn't."

"What was the second?"

"The second was a call-back *explaining* the mistake."

"And the third?" said George. "I mean, since you seem to have everything sorted out so well."

"The third was a charming call," said Jenny. "That was yours."

"True enough," said George. "Have you ever considered trying out for *Let's Make A Deal* or *Name That Tune?* You have a good mind, Jenny MacLaine. Now you see why you got the charming call."

"Really? That's the first time I've ever captivated anyone with my mind," said Jenny.

"See that?" said George. "All along you've had no one to appreciate your intellectual endowments."

"Intellectu—Well! You're a writer, that's for sure. This is what they call 'repartee,' isn't it?"

"No," said George. "Not in the strict sense. This is what they call 'amusing telephone conversation under duress.'"

"What's the duress?"

"I've just consumed a takeout portion of MSG. I believe that's the physiological equivalent of thirty-five Darvons."

"Should I call an ambulance?"

"No, no," said George. "I'd be embarrassed if the attendants saw the apartment. I haven't had a chance to clean. Of course, even when I have a chance, I don't do it." He paused. "Uh, in case you didn't know, I'm a widower."

"Yes. Faye told me."

"Faye?"

"Faye Medwick. She's the one pushing from my side."

"Leo is getting up a brochure on me. We'll send you one when they come in. I think he's taken a full-page ad in this Sunday's *Times*."

"I'll watch for it."

"Did, uh, I call you at a bad time?" asked George.

"I was just eating a salad and reading *Catch-22*," said Jenny.

"Which do you like better?"

"The salad," she answered quickly. "I once dated someone like Yossarian."

"Listen," said George, "I still have some Chinese food here. Why don't we take a quick dinner break?"

"What?" Jenny was confused. Was he asking her over for dinner? For leftovers?

"You know," said George. "Two spoonfuls each when I say 'go.'"

"Oh, I see. Fine. Okay."

"You ready?"

"Yes."

"Go."

74

He quickly shoveled in several heaping mounds of duck, rice, and sauce. He heard chewing sounds from the other end. "I cheated," he admitted after swallowing. "I took about seven spoonfuls instead of two."

"I took nine," said Jenny.

"Yours sounded better than mine," lied George. He looked down at the notepaper, now thoroughly stained by duck sauce. "Next to your number, Leo wrote 'divorcée.'"

"He's very thorough, isn't he?" said Jenny. "Did he list my measurements also? How about my social security number, or blood type?"

George was enjoying the sound of her voice. "I don't know if you've noticed," he said, "but we also talk in the same rhythm."

"Oh?"

"Oh? What's 'oh'?"

"It's second cousin to 'aha.'"

"Wouldn't you know it? It turns out we're related," said George.

"Listen, you're a very interesting telephone person, Mr. Schneider—"

"George."

"George," repeated Jenny.

"You may as well call me George," said George. "I've got forty cents invested in this relationship."

"George," said Jenny, "I am really exhausted. And despite the charming call-back, which really was charming, I just don't have the inclination to be equally endearing. Maybe some other time."

"Look," said George, "I really am sorry if—"

"Good-bye, George." She hung up.

This time it was George who felt slightly let down. He finished the rest of the Chinese food, then cleaned up the table. It was 10:00 P.M. He walked into the living room and switched on the Channel Five News. He watched blankly as the reports came in. New OPEC oil price rises. New York City budget debt much larger than expected. Brooklyn fire kills three. Man falls to death off IRT subway platform. A disaster parade. Gabe interviews Mayor Koch, Mazur with sports, Linda with weather, Stu reviews a new movie. Same old horrors, thought George. He changed channels, found a Knick game, and became immersed in the action. He dribbled across mid-court with Earl, passed to Ray Williams at the top of the key, crosscourted to Toby Knight, and went up for the jump shot. Score! George leaped to his feet. Sports. Pure and sweet. A simplification and reduction of life. He watched intently for a half hour, totally involved in the action, and by the halftime break he was drained. His clothes were soaked with perspiration. At the phone, sweat ran into his eyes as he dialed.

"Hello?" he said.

"It couldn't be," said Jenny.

"Were you sleeping?" asked George.

"Soundly, thank you."

"I'm sorry. You usually go to bed this early?"

"When I come from another time zone, yes. What is it now?"

"About ten-thirty."

"I meant, what is it you want?"

"I was thinking," said George.

"This is why you woke me?"

"We really should be practical," he continued. "They're not going to let up, you know."

"Who?"

"The pushers."

76

"The—Ah, you mean Leo and Faye," said Jenny.

"Yes. They will persist and push and prod and leave telephone numbers on scraps of paper until we have that inevitable date."

"Nothing is inevitable," said Jenny sleepily. "Dates are man-made."

"Why do you suppose matchmaking for unattached friends seems to be such a strong drive?" asked George. "You think it's in the genes?"

"I don't think jeans have anything to do with it," said Jenny. "I'm sure it's been going on since way before they were popular."

"Aha!" said George. "Excellent. Seriously, though, you think it could be some kind of natural adaptation response, like when primitive men stood upright millions of years ago to see over the tall grasses of the savanna? Or when the amphibians crawled out of the drying Devonian swamps?"

Jenny yawned and lay back on the pillow. "As I understand it," she said, "those all led to evolutionary advances. I doubt very much if that's the case here."

"You think, then, that this is one of nature's blind alleys?"

"Could be."

"Damn!"

"You dislike blind alleys?" asked Jenny.

"No, not especially."

"Then why the 'damn'?"

"Oh. That's just the game. They've resumed after intermission, and the Bullets scored the first basket."

"You mean, you've been watching TV while we've been talking?"

"Let's just say it was on. Anyway, the Knicks are down by twelve."

"Now I *really* won't sleep," said Jenny.

"And after I worked so hard in the first half," said George.

"Rooting?"

"Yes. Sort of. More than that, actually. Anyway, my point before was, you apparently have an active career, and I can't work with Leo bugging me all the time. So I propose, in the interest of moving on with our lives, that we get this meeting over with just as soon as possible."

"Surely you jest," said Jenny. "You mean we should meet, not because we want to, but to get two other people off our backs?"

"It's a reason," said George.

"It's a lousy reason," said Jenny.

"All right," said George. "Look, hear me out. What if we were to meet for just five minutes?"

Jenny, awake now, began to smile at the absurdity of all this.

"We could say hello," George went on, "look each other over, then part company."

"To what end?"

"To no end! The whole point would be that we could then tell Leo and Faye that they have performed their noble missions in life."

"We could tell them that without meeting."

"But that would be lying. I hate to lie."

"But wouldn't we just be offering up a verbal facade of truth while sabotaging their honest intentions?"

"You have a nice way of expressing yourself, Jenny."

"Wouldn't we?"

"Well . . . yes."

"That's very funny," said Jenny.

"And yet I hear no laughter," said George.

"Because I don't think it's funny."

On TV, the Knicks were asking for a time-out.

"Listen," Jenny continued, "can I call you right back?"

"You also want time-out?"

Jenny didn't get the reference and decided to ignore it. "I have to take two aspirins, I've got a terrible headache."

"That's okay," said George. "I'll call *you* back."

Jenny could not trust him; the man was crazy. No doubt he *would* call back, but it might be three or four in the morning.

"No," she said. "Please. That's why I have the headache. Give me a few minutes."

"Take all the time you want," said George. "If you should wish to schedule your call between the third and fourth periods, of course, you'll find me a bit more relaxed."

"You're talking about the basketball game?"

"Yes."

"I have no competence in that area. All periods of a basketball game look alike to me, as do all the interludes."

"Okay," said George. "Just a thought."

"What's your number?"

George gave it to her. "This is getting exciting, isn't it?"

"No."

She hung up. She really did have a headache now, although she hadn't before. She climbed off the bed, crossed into the kitchen alcove, and downed two aspirins with a glass of water. Magically, her headache seemed to vanish. Psychosomatic, she thought. Self-induced. It was not unusual with her. She was one of those people on whom placebos worked wonders; she got crushing chest pains after reading an obituary column. Suggestible, in all respects. Two vitamin C tablets could instantly halt a raging cold. Skin creams made rashes vanish overnight. Fodder for the faith healers, she thought. Her subconscious would believe anything. She tapped out George's number on one of her few luxuries, a push-button phone.

"Listen," said George, "you can't keep calling me like this." He felt better; the Knicks had cut the Bullet lead to six.

"I'm sorry," said Jenny. "I lost my head."

"So what do you think?"

"I think you can't be serious."

"A quick five-minute hello and good-bye?" said George. "Two speedboats passing in the night?"

"I don't like boats."

"All right, trains then? Burros? Pick your own vehicle."

"Whatever the vehicle, it's equivalent to shopping."

"So choose shopping carts. We'll meet like two shopping carts in the night. Rendezvous at the supermarket."

"I like shopping even less than boats," said Jenny. "And I particularly don't wish to *be* shopped."

"How about through a window?" said George. "I could stand across the street, look up, and wave?"

"Am I talking to a competent person?"

"My friends tell me I do have a certain charm,"

said George. "It's like gold, though. You have to pan for it."

"How do I know your friends are reliable? Some people will say anything."

"My friends will say anything," said George, "but they're also reliable." On the TV, the Knicks committed a costly foul.

"And what if," said Jenny, "during these five minutes we took a liking to each other?"

"Then we take a shot at six minutes."

"But if you take a fancy to me, and I don't to you—or, God forbid, vice versa—what then?"

"We agree to binding arbitration."

"Who?"

"Leo."

"No good."

"Theodore Kheel. Ralph Nader. Anyone reasonable."

"You want Ralph Nader to decide whether we should date or not?" asked Jenny.

"Well . . . he could at least tell us if it's safe."

Jenny shook her head. "I think we have a problem here."

"It's a new system," said George. "We don't have all the bugs out yet."

Jenny's headache was beginning to return. "I can't believe this conversation."

"Maybe you're dreaming it," suggested George. "Or maybe I've fallen asleep in front of the TV, and I'm dreaming it."

"I wouldn't dream this type of thing," said Jenny. "Weird phone calls are not part of my repertoire."

"It must be me then," said George. "They're in mine." The Knicks had fallen behind by twelve again, and the third quarter was over. He had an idea. "Look, if five minutes is too exhausting, we could have two-and-a-half-minute halves, with an intermission."

Jenny, despite herself, was grinning. The whole thing was so inane. "Why am I intrigued by this?" she said.

"The old human desire to watch someone make a fool of himself, I expect," said George. For the first time, he became more interested in the conversation than the game.

"When did you want this momentous meeting to take place?" asked Jenny softly.

George felt a tiny thrill of excitement. "How about tomorrow night? From 7:10 to 7:15?"

"I hate Leo and Faye," said Jenny.

"Most people don't hate Leo till they get to know him," said George. "Still, I suppose it doesn't hurt to have a head start."

"Where did you want to meet?" asked Jenny.

"I don't know," said George. The fourth quarter of the game had begun. "You know a restaurant where I can book a table for five minutes?"

"Make it my place," said Jenny decisively. She gave him the address.

"I have it," said George, trying to concentrate.

"Write it down," demanded Jenny. "You have a bad history with numbers."

"Why?" said George. "It's a lucky thing I got you. Serena Jurgens and I could have been a hot item by now."

Jenny couldn't help giggling. "Listen, you don't think this is a weird thing to do?"

"Mystical," said George. "A bit eerie. 'Weird' makes it seem too odd. It's not that odd. It seems to me this is a natural follow-up to the latest computer dating service. You know, the one where they let you see a video tape of the other person. Well, this is the next step. Live. Beyond tape. The minidate. A free sample, if you will. I think of us as pioneers. We may be blazing the trail for millions of others."

"Or ruining it."

"I don't see how."

"I guess . . ." said Jenny. "And neither of us will be disappointed if we're disappointed?"

"Please . . ." said George.

"It has to be considered. There are possibilities."

"Let's not build down our hopes too much," said George. "I'll see you tomorrow, okay? I'll be wearing a cow mask and metal shoes, so you'll know who it is. Good-bye."

"Good-bye," said Jenny.

She hung up. No matter what he says, she thought, it *is* weird.

6

George wore blue pants that were tight in the waist and a Dacron shirt with the top two buttons open. The taxi smelled from Old Spice, with which he had inundated himself just before leaving his apartment. The last thing he had done was to tease several chest hairs out where they'd be visible. Of course, he was being ridiculous and hardly acting his age, but who was to know? He felt, for some reason, more nervous than he'd been on his previous Leo-arranged dates. It seemed more important that he impress this girl. Was it her obvious intelligence, he wondered, a fear that she'd be discriminating enough to reject him? Did he have to feel superior to a woman to relax in her presence? It seemed a likely answer, and he preferred not to explore the implications.

The cab got stalled in the evening crosstown traffic.

"You a stockbroker?" asked the driver, a short black man with a broad face and graying hair.

"Not me," said George. "Do I look like one?"

"Could be," said the driver. "You got that men's perfume, like they all wears."

"Mmm," said George.

"Ah once bought mahse'f a stock," the cabbie said. "Name of it were General Fruit. Ah boughts it 'cause ah like fruit."

"How'd it do?"

The driver shrugged. "Never did find out."

"Didn't you look in the papers?" George asked.

"Yep. Ah try, but I can't fin' nothin'."

"Your stock isn't listed?"

"Nope."

"It's over-the-counter then," suggested George.

"Weren't over no counter neither," said the driver, making an illegal left turn. "Ah bought it direc' from Rib."

"Who's Rib?"

"Mah broker," said the cabbie. "Live up on one-eighteenth street."

"Who's he with?" asked George.

"He live by hisself. He ain' with no one."

"No, I mean his firm," said George. "Like Bache, or Merrill Lynch, or E. F. Hutton."

"It just Rib," said the cabbie, smiling. He shook his head. "Man, you sure don' know much about stocks."

"I guess not," said George.

"Rib, he make big money fo' people. You treats him right, you walk away with three, fo' hun'red dollar."

"That's what you expect on your General Fruit?"

"Damn right," said the driver. "Rib say, 'You give me twenty-eight bucks, you come out fine.' An' ah believe the man. Ah seed the way he live."

"How long ago was this?" asked George.

"'Bout six, seven years," said the cabbie. He turned as they stopped for a light. "But ah ain' worried none, case thass what you thinkin'. Rib, he give me good advice. Say, 'Don' never inves' mo' than you kin 'ford to lose.' Then he ask, 'How much you kin 'ford to lose?' an' ah say, 'Twenty-eight dollar.' So thass what ah gives him."

"Well, it sounds like he offers good advice," said George, "but I'd check up anyway."

"You suspicious."

"In general, yes."

"You some kinda welfare worker or somethin'? An investigator?"

George chuckled. "A writer," he said. "I write books."

"That so?" said the driver. "That take a lotta brains."

"Well . . ." said George.

"Mah son aim for writin'," said the cabbie. "Took one of them New School classes, but he say he couldn't git the hang of it. Teacher kep' markin' up his papers with red, you know?"

"Some instructors like to show off," said George.

"He want to drop out, mah boy," said the cabbie, "but ah tells him, you keep pluggin', keep grindin' away. Otherwise you end up like your Daddy, drivin' some broken-down hack."

"Sure," said George, feeling suddenly quite depressed. "Let him keep at it."

At two minutes past seven, the cab pulled over to the curb in front of Jenny's brownstone. The fare was four dollars and sixty cents. For reasons he did not understand, George left a three dollar tip.

• • • •

87

Jenny stood by the window, staring down into the street. She was wearing tight black pants and a beige silk blouse, which she alternately tucked in and then pulled out. She had gained a tiny bit of weight in the last week and, as usual, it concentrated in her stomach. With the blouse tucked in, a careful side view revealed the beginning of a small potbelly. With the blouse out, however, it seemed that she was trying to *hide* the beginning of a small potbelly. Girdles and related garments were out; to wear a girdle was to acknowledge a problem, which Jenny refused to do. Seven pounds were simply not a problem. They could be dieted off in a week and a half—if one had the willpower. She finally decided on blouse *in*. Better a small imperfection, she thought, than the appearance of concealment. *She,* at least, had learned something from Watergate. Besides, some men, she'd heard, actually liked small bellies, found the soft roundness pleasing, feminine. She watched George get out of the cab. I've gone crazy, she thought. I don't even know this guy. What the hell do I care what he thinks? She pulled the back of the blouse out of the pants. The phone rang just as George crossed to the curb. She answered it.

"Hi, Jenny."

"Faye," she said, "I can't talk to you now. He's on his way up."

"Who is?"

"George Schneider."

"You mean—"

"Yes, *your* George Schneider."

"He asked for a date?"

"It's not a date, it's a look."

"It's what?"

88

"I'll call you back in five minutes," said Jenny. "Because that's all a look takes."

She hung up and raced to the mirror for a quick hair comb. She heard a scuffing sound outside the door and then the ring of the bell. She cleared her throat.

"Who is it?" she said musically.

"The Five Minute Man."

Jenny unlatched the chain, then opened the main lock. For a moment she and George simply stared at each other.

"Yeah!" he said. "Oka-a-ay!"

"Is that a review?" she asked.

"No, just a response." He smiled. "Hello."

"Hello." She kept looking at him. "You're taller than your voice."

"I'm not what you expected?"

"Well, you know, you form a certain picture. . . Yours was pudgier and shorter."

"Yours is perfect," said George.

Jenny chuckled, more from awkwardness than amusement.

"I think I put a lot of pressure on these next five minutes," said George.

"You could cut it with a knife."

"I think if I came in, it would lessen the tension," said George. He glanced back into the hallway.

"Yes, please," said Jenny. "By all means, do come in."

George entered, and she closed the door behind him. "Aha!" he said, looking around.

"Does that mean you comprehend my apartment?"

"No. It means I like it."

"I thought it meant comprehension."

"'Aha' is versatile," said George. "It's like *nu* in Yiddish. You know Yiddish?"

"No."

"Well, 'Aha' can be used in many situations, such as buying a little time to get over opening jitters. Some people may say 'Oho,' although most scholars consider that a variant."

"What would the scholars think of a little white wine?"

"I believe they'd consider it quite mainstream," said George.

"Good," said Jenny. "Please . . . sit down."

She padded over to the kitchen alcove. George sprawled on the sofa and surveyed the room. "Is it all right if I pry?" he asked. "Occupational hazard."

"Be my guest," called Jenny from behind the refrigerator door. From the bottom shelf, she removed a bottle of *Chenon Blanc*, Robert Mondavi, 1975. "I understand," she added. "I generally motivate too much."

George's eye fastened on a picture of a football player, partially hidden behind a lamp on one of the end tables. It was one of those posed snapshots that pretend to be candid, the man ostensibly caught in mid-stride, ball tucked in one hand, other arm held out stiffly to ward off tacklers. The face, where it peeked out from the helmet, was pinched and worried looking; it was not the face of a star.

"You a football fan?" he asked.

"That's my ex-husband," said Jenny.

"No kidding," said George. "This a college photo or something?"

"Pro," called Jenny, who was struggling with a

90

corkscrew. Somehow, every time she opened a bottle she managed to push the cork inside. "He was a wide receiver for the New York Giants."

"Wow," said George. "I'm impressed. What's his name?"

"Gus Hendricks." Jenny moistened the corkscrew before starting again.

"Gus Hendricks," repeatd George. "Gus Hendricks. Funny, I can't remember him. How wide a receiver was he?"

Jenny let her memory drift back. She was a young actress-model and Gus was a second-round draft choice. They'd met at Bachelors II, Joe Namath's place. Gus was soft-spoken, naive, a gorgeous physical specimen. They had dated on and off for three months, were married in early September during the exhibition season. He had plans: six years in pro ball, then a job in broadcasting, then coaching at a major college. He'd been All-Pro at Penn; everyone said he had the size, the speed, to make it really big. With a pretty, young actress-wife, the two of them would sweep New York, do commercials together, be invited to the poshest parties. It was a marriage built on shared dreams.

"He was cut the beginning of his second year," said Jenny. The cork plunged into the bottle. She filled two crystal glasses with wine. "Bad hands, I think they call it," she added as she returned to the living room. She handed George a glass.

"Shame," said George.

"Couldn't hold on to the football."

"Well, some coaches are very demanding. What does he do now?"

Mopes and sulks, thought Jenny. The endless aftermath of falling apart. Gus had disintegrated; he could not accept defeat. A life of continual successes and ever-greater achievement simply did not prepare one for reversals. There was no emotional base to fall back on, no philosophy to establish perspective. The bigger you blow up a balloon, Jenny would tell friends afterwards, the louder the bang when it's punctured. Gus had been punctured. For months after his dismissal, he'd been nearly comatose, sprawled all day on the living room couch while Jenny went in search of jobs. The next summer he applied to five other teams, was invited to training camp by the Colts, was cut again after a week. He played two games of semipro ball in the fall, then abruptly quit. "The lockers," he told Jenny tearfully. "They don't even have enough lockers. You have to share."

Gus tried to change careers, found himself prepared for nothing. He was unable to concentrate. The high point of Gus Hendricks's life had occurred when he was an undergraduate. The rest would all be epilogue. Of course, their marriage fell apart.

"He was in mutual funds," said Jenny. "He was a partner in a saloon. He was in broadcasting for a while, sports promotion . . ."

"Very ambitious," said George.

"He did all those things in three months."

"I gather, then, that he bores easily."

"Fails easily." Jenny looked down and shook her head. "That was unfair," she added.

"No one says you have to be fair."

"Maybe someday he'll find himself," said Jenny. "Come to terms." She shrugged. "He has some problems to work out."

"Who doesn't?" said George.

"True enough." She raised her glass. "Well . . . here's to working out problems, yes?"

"Indeed." They both drank. "Really good," said George. "South side of the vineyard, I should judge."

"Is that right?" said Jenny. "I don't know the first thing about wines. I can't even open a bottle without pushing in the cork."

"I don't know anything either," said George. "That was a joke. Leo told me once that if I commented on the vineyard people would assume I was a *maven*. The thing is, I think you have to know *when* to comment."

"Could've fooled me," said Jenny. She saw that he was watching her.

"Leo was right," said George.

"He must drink a lot of wine."

"I mean about you. You're very attractive."

Jenny flushed. "Thank you."

"I'm curious," said George. "You don't have to answer this. . . . How was *I* described?"

" 'Not gorgeous, but an intelligent face.' "

George nodded. "That's true. I have. You can ask my face anything."

Jenny seated herself next to him and sipped the wine. "I hope it's not too chilled," she said. "I never know how cold to make it."

"It's fine," said George. He inhaled. "I like your perfume."

"I may have overdone it," said Jenny.

"Not at all."

"I didn't know how much to put on for five minutes."

"You did as well with the perfume as you did

with the wine," said George. "Both are exquisite."

"Beginner's luck," said Jenny.

George was staring at his knees. "You think this was a dumb thing to do?"

Jenny shrugged. "I thought so three minutes ago."

"And now?"

"Now I'm getting the hang of it."

George stood up, almost spilling his wine. Clumsy nit, he thought. "It was an idea born out of fear," he said.

"Fear has motivated some of humanity's greatest achievements," said Jenny.

"And some of its worst," said George. "How often is necessity the mother of calamity?"

Jenny smiled briefly. "Do you write the way you talk?"

"Oh, this isn't talking," said George. "This is impressing. Talking comes soon."

"Good!" said Jenny cheerfully. "Now . . . tell me . . . what were the others like?"

"What others?"

"The girls Leo arranged."

George glanced at the ceiling. "Oh, like a walk down Eighth Avenue at two in the morning. Hooker heaven, I guess you'd call it."

"Really . . ."

"Well, let's see. There was Bambi. I think her income went into six figures the year the Democratic Convention was in town. And Kitten. She—"

"Kitten?"

"Yes. As in immature feline. I'm not certain how she made a living, but all I know is that she used to come to our dates in a Caddy driven by a man in a mink coat and wide-brimmed hat."

"I get the picture."

"Then there was Vilma. A dynamite girl."

"Oh . . . well, at least she sounds a little different."

"She was. Spent three years in a Turkish prison for carrying dynamite. Told me she got out by helping the guards to relieve their aggressions." George paused. "Should I go on?"

Jenny held up a hand. "I think I've had enough."

"So did I," he said. "Since then I've decided to take everything Leo says with a grain of panic, or at least two aspirin." He drained the wine and placed the glass on the coffee table. "That's why I'm so surprised."

"In what way?" said Jenny. It was a mild fish for compliments, she knew, but he seemed eager to pay them.

"Well . . . that here I find myself with an attractive, intelligent, and what appears to be a very nice girl."

"Thank you," said Jenny. "You're very flattering."

"I meant to be."

"I really enjoyed talking to you on the phone," said Jenny. "You're very bright."

"I study," said George.

"I found I had to stay on my toes to keep up with you," said Jenny.

"Is that unusual?"

"I haven't been off my heels in years."

George chuckled, then fell silent. For several seconds neither of them spoke.

"First awkward moment of silence," he said at last. "Not bad for three minutes."

"I didn't think it was awkward," said Jenny. "I thought it was rather skillful. Appropriate. Just right."

George nodded. "I'll agree it didn't compare with the eighteen-minute gap in the Nixon tape, but as for skillful . . . well, I wouldn't quite go that far."

Jenny shrugged. "I could fill it in with food. Would you like some cheese?"

"Perfect time for cheese."

She went back into the kitchen, and George followed. He sat down at the tiny, two-person table while she took a wedge of Muenster from the refrigerator and placed it on a small wooden serving board. "Voila!" she said, offering George a knife from the drying rack on the sink.

"Gus Hendricks," said George. "Now I remember."

"Crackers," said Jenny. "I'll get you some crackers." She found a box in a closet and spread a few crackers on the board next to the cheese.

"Second-round draft pick," said George. "I remember now. Wasn't that the year they got Tucker Fredrickson and Ernie Koy?"

"Gus came later," said Jenny. "But left before."

"Dropped three touchdown passes against the Rams," said George. "I remember the game. The field was covered with snow."

"It was the Vikings," said Jenny.

"Oh, yeah . . . right. The Vikings."

"And it was two touchdown passes. The other was a fumble on an end-around play."

George shook his head. "I remember the pictures in the paper the next day. You know, the locker room, him with his head down. As I recall, he was never heard from again."

"There, you are correct," said Jenny. "At least *I* certainly didn't hear much from him." Her attempt at glibness didn't work; even she could discern the bitterness in her voice.

George sliced off a piece of cheese. A cracker crumbled in his hand. His eyes met hers. "I'm forty-two years old," he said carefully, and waited for the reaction.

"Today?"

"What? Oh, no. No. I mean in general."

"I see."

"That doesn't bother you?"

Jenny nibbled on some Muenster. "I don't understand. Your reference to your age—is that a statement of some historic importance?"

"No," said George. "I just wanted you to know."

"But why?"

He smiled at her coyness. "Because you look to be in your late twenties, and I feel like I'm acting about seventeen, and I didn't want you to think I was too young for you."

"I'm thirty-four," said Jenny. "And I like younger men." She paused. "I also like older men."

"Thirty-four," echoed George. "Thirty-four. That was a good year for women."

"No, no, I wasn't born in 'thirty-four. I meant I *am* thirty-four."

"I know that," said George. "I was just musing." He was conscious of how close they were in the tiny kitchen. Her perfume had begun to mix with her natural body scents, and he found himself becoming intoxicated with the aroma. "I— There's one more thing," he said.

"Shoot."

"I mean, as long as we're making a quick but incisive survey here."

"Fire away."

"I mean, it's not important to me, but it may be to you."

"Let it hang out."

George choked briefly on a cracker. "I'm . . . Je—I'm—Je—Je—" His eyes watered. "Jewish," he gasped out.

Jenny opened her own eyes wide in mock horror and crammed a fist into her mouth.

George stopped choking and began to laugh.

"That *is* a shocker," said Jenny finally. "But I can adapt. *Macht nichts* to me."

"*Nisht,*" said George. "*Nicht* is German. *Nisht* is Yiddish. But either way, I'm glad to hear it."

"I'm glad you're glad."

George paused, then raised his eyebrows. "So?"

"So?"

"So what do you think?"

"About what?"

"About me."

Jenny chuckled. "You really like to come right to the point, don't you?"

"I'm not always this direct," said George, "but we're fighting the clock."

Jenny nodded with theatrical gravity. "My hunch," she said, "is that you're a very interesting person, George."

"Well, my advice is—play your hunches."

Jenny pursed her lips. "Shall we have some more wine?" She grabbed the bottle from the sink top where she'd left it and headed for the living room, George trailing behind. At the coffee table, she bent to pour.

"None for me, thanks," said George. It took superb self-control. He would have liked very much to linger, to be with this woman, even to hug her, even to make love to her—but now wasn't the time. He'd done well; he'd seen, shown himself to good advantage (he thought), had played it cool. Now was the time to back off, to distance himself, to evaluate. But damn . . . it was difficult. "I think I better be going," he said.

"Oh? Time's up?"

"I don't need any more."

Jenny swallowed. "Is that good, or bad?"

"Well . . . good, I guess. I mean, I know what my next move is."

"Really."

"Yes."

"Can you tell?"

"Certainly," said George. "I'd like to make a regulation date."

"Ah, so. International rules?"

"Seven to twelve, your basic normal hours."

Jenny was relieved. For a moment, her confidence had wavered. And she did want to see this man again. "You mean with grown-up clothes and makeup?"

"Bath, shower, everything."

"You really think we're ready for the big time?"

"Opportunity knocks but once," said George.

"Although you should look before you leap," said Jenny.

"I have looked," said George. "I'm ready to leap. Uh, figuratively, that is."

"It wouldn't be so terrible if it was literally."

"All right, maybe that too. But for the moment, the operative word is restraint. We just had four minutes in the minor leagues, we're ready to move up."

Jenny banged her fist lightly on the table. "Okay!"

"Done?"

"Done."

"Agreed?"

"Why not? Let's make it," said Jenny.

"Terrific," said George. "What's today?"

"Tuesday."

"How about Wednesday?"

"Let me consult my calendar," said Jenny. She paused. "I just remembered, I don't have a calendar." She giggled. "I think Wednesday works out well."

"You could play hard to get."

"I thought I was. Otherwise I would've suggested the rest of tonight."

"I like a girl who's forthright," said George. "I meant we could make it Thursday."

"No," said Jenny. "Let's stick with Wednesday, and I'll keep you waiting half an hour."

"Fair enough."

They walked to the door, and George turned. "This . . . was nice," he said.

"Yes . . ."

"I'm glad we met, Jenny."

"So am I, George."

He grinned and shook his head. "I can't believe you're from the same man who gave us Bambi and Vilma," he said. He waved and started down the hall.

7

They sat in Nirvana, an Indian restaurant high above Central Park. Sitar music played discordantly in the background while George tried to explain how he'd become a writer.

"I was fired," he said.

"From what?" asked Jenny. She sat looking out at the night-lit Manhattan. She wore a simple silk dress, fairly low-cut.

"Advertising," said George. "I had an MBA from NYU, but nothing interested me; business was easy. I worked for McCann and Benton, very progressive firm. I hung out with the creative guys; they told good jokes. I had three-martini lunches with minor clients. After three martinis, I have the perceptual abilities of a doorknob. Still, my boss seemed to like me. I was pleasant, diffident, apologetic. I think my greatest asset, though, was a certain cultivated anonymity. It was a sort of blandness I'd developed in college, an ability to avoid notice, to blend in. It's quite possible I would've been fired earlier, it's just that no one remembered I was there."

"I can't understand that," said Jenny.

A waiter came with their bread. George had ordered three different kinds. "One is from the lowlands," the waiter had explained. "Very tangy. Distinctive. The other is an ancient recipe, served only to the nobles, for generations. The last is found mainly in the North, quite popular with Sikhs."

George sampled chunks of the breads. They tasted exactly alike. "Then, one day," he continued, "my boss was touring executives of the firm's largest client around the company. I didn't know. When they came into my office, I had my feet on the desk, shoes off, picking sock lint from between my toes. I got three weeks' severance."

"It doesn't sound as if you were too devastated," said Jenny.

"Devastated? No. But don't let anyone tell you he just shrugged off being fired. It still hurts, even if you hate the job. No one likes being judged unfit, even if the judge is—pardon me—an asshole."

"And so then you just began writing books?" asked Jenny.

"I looked for another job," said George, "only this time, I knew I wasn't going to stay there. I found a position with an employment agency, and lunchtimes, evenings, weekends, I started doing character sketches. Three- or four-page descriptions of people I'd known. Some of them were quite funny, others we're just nasty, bitter. Six months later I tried my first short story. Take one guess what it was about."

"An unhappy guy who works in an employment agency?" said Jenny.

George grinned. "On the money. I decided to send it out to magazines. I was positive it would sell. I *knew* it would sell. I sent it to the *New Yorker*." He paused. "What happens now?"

102

"You get it back with a form rejection."

George chuckled. "Wrong! It sold! The *New Yorker* actually bought it. It was crazy. I wasn't even surprised. I figured that's the way it was supposed to be. I wrote another story. The *New Yorker* liked it, but decided to pass. I sent it to *McCall's*. Don't ask me why *McCall's*, I just did."

"And they bought it?

"Yes. Amazing. I, of course, reacted very coolly and intelligently.

Jenny nodded. "You quit your job."

George raised his eyebrows. "Here it is, an hour into our first date, and you already know me like a book."

"It was a guess," said Jenny.

The waiter came with their salads.

"Am I talking too much?" asked George. "I mean, I have this tendency to go off the deep end. When you asked me how I became a writer, I'll bet you weren't expecting a doctoral dissertation."

"No, no, I'm interested," said Jenny. "Believe me, I'm not shy. You'd know it if I was bored. But go on. Now you've quit your job."

"Yes. I knock off five more stories in the next three months. I'm living off savings and payments from my first sales. And now, of course, I can't sell anything. I try the stories at about twenty magazines each, and no one buys. From the *New Yorker* I get apologetic letters; at *McCall's*, my editor left, I get nothing. I decided short stories were impossible, that one sale had no bearing on the next, that you couldn't live on the proceeds anyway. I came to the conclusion I had to be a novelist."

"That was a pretty gutsy decision."

"It was made in ignorance. I had the courage of

103

the totally uninformed. Anyway, I started a book. Six months went by. My money was gone. Leo, my beautiful Leo, is keeping me alive. He invites me three times a week for dinner, slips a ten into my pocket whenever he can. 'My contribution to the arts,' he says. I slog away at the typewriter. And then, funds completely gone, I make another careful, thought-out maneuver."

George looked at Jenny, but her face remained blank.

"I get married," George explained. "I'd been seeing Barbara for some time. I was at my lowest ebb; broke, down on myself, three-quarters through a novel whose point I was losing . . . and I needed someone to give me comfort and solace. Thank God she accepted my proposal. At that point one more rejection would've finished me off."

"But I guess somehow you managed," said Jenny.

"I managed," agreed George. "I finished the book, and Leo showed it to a literary agent he knew. It was a semiautobiography, as you might expect—sincere, funny in parts, lacking in form and technique. The agent's name was William Warren, and he invited me up to his apartment, which was in Brooklyn, on Flatbush Avenue. I remember the carpeting was very worn, and the furniture was old, and you could see dust in the air whenever any sunlight happened to filter into the living room. Warren and I talked for about an hour, and then he asked if I'd like him to represent me. He was an old guy, in his sixties, I guess, and very skinny. He wore a bow tie that bobbed on his Adam's apple whenever he spoke. On the walls were pictures of writers he'd handled, and some of them I recognized. 'You still represent Styron?' I asked. 'Not anymore,' he said. 'How about Price?' 'He left about three years ago.' 'And Hersey?' 'Not since 1950.' I nodded. What could I do? I really didn't want to have an agent with threadbare carpeting and a bow tie, but it would've gone against all my humane instincts to refuse him. I said yes. Two weeks after, he sold my novel to Doubleday. I later found out he's a multimillionaire and rarely meets clients in person. He has thirty people working in his Manhattan office."

"He's still your agent?" asked Jenny.

"Absolutely."

"And how'd the book do?"

George tilted his head. "It was what they call an 'artistic success.' Same thing with my second book. 'Artistic success' means 'write more, but not too soon.'"

"They didn't make much money, I gather," said Jenny.

"Well, together with Barbara's salary, we had one salary."

"They didn't go into paperback?"

"The second one did. It sold about a thousand books, I think, most of them to Leo. The good thing was that at the paperback company I met one of the copywriters whom I'd known from McCann and Benton. He'd become an editor since, and he remembered me. He asked me if I wanted to do hackwork for good money."

"You mean sell out?"

"He didn't put it that way . . . but yes. Naturally, I agreed immediately."

"The spy novels?"

"Yes. I write them under the name of Kenneth Blakely Hyphen Hill."

"Hyphen Hill?"

"You don't say the hyphen, you just put it in."

The waiter came with silver-covered dishes and placed them on the table. Jenny had ordered curried chicken; George, a specially spiced fish.

"Careful," said the waiter. "Very hot. Thank you. Enjoy meal."

They uncovered their dishes. "Who picked the name?" asked Jenny.

"Barbara," said George. "Spy novels sell better when they sound English. We spent some time in the Catskills at a place called the Blakely Hotel. It was on a hill, and the busboy's name was Kenneth." He shrugged. "If we'd had money in those days, I might have been Kenneth Waldorf-Astoria."

Jenny had been mulling the name. "Blakely-Hill, Blakely-Hill . . . my God. Yes! I've seen it. But . . . you're very popular. In airports and drugstores and—"

"Unfortunately, not in libraries," said George. He stared down at his plate. "What did we pick here? It looks like something from *Mutiny on the Bounty*."

Jenny was delicately chewing a piece of chicken. "It's *very* spicy. Maybe we should have ordered everything mild."

"No problem," said George jauntily. "There's a fire station three blocks away." He put a forkful of fish in his mouth. "So . . . tell me more about you now. You said you've been in some plays."

Jenny swallowed. "God, you name it. Two years with the Shakespeare Festival in Stratford. *The Little Foxes* and *A Doll's House* at the Beaumont.

Major Barb—" She stopped. George's eyes were not blinking. "You okay?"

He nodded stiffly.

"*Major Barbara*," she continued uncertainly. "Then there were three Broadway plays that never got to Broadway, if you don't count Circle in the Square. . . ." George was beet-faced now, his neck muscles rigid, veins standing out on his forehead.

"Are you sure you're all right?" asked Jenny.

This time he shook his head no.

"Is it too spicy?"

He nodded, placed a napkin to his mouth.

"Are you in pain?"

He nodded again, pointed to his streaming eyes.

"Your eyes are tearing?"

More nods.

"Oh, I'm sorry, George," said Jenny. "Mine is hot, but not *that* hot. Why don't you spit it out in the napkin?"

George shook his head. .

"It's too late? You've already swallowed it?"

"Mmm," said George. He reached for his glass of water, finished it, then drank Jenny's. After a moment he sat back, opened his mouth, and loosened his tie.

"Would some bread help?" asked Jenny.

"Nothing," whispered George, "could help. Just a little time."

"You shouldn't have let me recommend the restaurant," said Jenny. "I went on hearsay evidence."

George was fanning his mouth. "It's a good thing the napkin is made of asbestos," he said.

Sometime later, at the waiter's suggestion, George received a replacement dish—"Very bland,

107

a favorite of the nineteenth-century maharajahs."
George sampled it carefully with his tongue. Not
surprisingly, it tasted exactly like the breads.

•   •   •   •

Their next date was two days later. A visit to
the Metropolitan Museum of Art, then downtown to
Rockefeller Center, stops in Saks, Henri Bendel's,
Sam Goody's, and finally, window shopping on
Spring street. They'd bought ice-cream cones. Jenny
had vanilla, George, Rocky Road.

"You sure you don't have to work today?" she
asked as they stood looking through a store window
at an elaborate display of dresses.

"My boss granted me some time off," said
George.

"You don't set yourself a certain goal each
day?"

"Sure I do," said George. "My typewriter's on
automatic. I leave it an idea, it writes it while I'm
out."

They stepped inside the store, a boutique
called Victoria Falls. There were half a dozen shop-
pers, three salesgirls. George was the only man. Jenny immediately selected two dresses and went into a
curtained booth to try them on. George sat in a
chair. There was a gap between the curtain and the
wooden side panel. Tantalizing glimpses of bared
legs and shoulders would occasionally appear, then
immediately vanish. After several moments George
began to go crazy. He stood up, walked to a rack of
dresses featuring sequins and frills. He pretended to
look at the merchandise, anything to keep his eyes
and mind off what was behind the curtains.

"Can I help you?" came a soft voice.

George glanced up. It was a salesgirl, black, attractive, in her early twenties. "Yeah," he said. "You got anything in a forty-two long?"

She blinked a bit more than usual, but otherwise showed no special reaction. Obviously, thought George, she was used to everything.

"I'm big across the shoulders," he elaborated.

"I don't know," she said. "Whatever's on the rack. You can look."

George nodded. A moment later Jenny emerged from the booth. She wore a three-quarter-length lace dress and a large Gibson Girl hat. She crossed to him with a model's walk, pausing to stop and turn. George smiled.

"You think I'd get much use out of this?" she asked.

"Not unless Mark Twain asks us to dinner."

The next day they toured the Village. At Jenny's insistence they stopped in a bookstore on Sixth Avenue near Ninth Street. They browsed for fifteen minutes before she pulled a heavy volume from a section marked "Discontinued Fiction."

"Here!" she yelled.

Several people glanced around. George padded over from where he'd been talking to the clerk near the front counter. "Where?"

"This," said Jenny, hefting the book. She read the spine: "Schneider. *The Glass Hat.* Is that it?"

George took the book, pointed to the front cover. "*Vivian* Schneider. Do I look like Vivian Schneider?"

The clerk from the front desk joined them. She was an elderly woman with a pronounced stoop. "I'm sorry," she said. "We have nothing in our back catalogue by a George Schneider. It's not one of those porno books, is it? We don't keep track of those."

"No," said George. "At least, I didn't intend it that way. Although one critic said it had no redeeming social value."

"Well, we don't have it," said the clerk. Her stoop required her to lean backward in order to look at him.

"That's okay," said George. "Thanks anyway."

"You're sure you're the author?"

"Why would I make something like that up?" said George.

"Too bad you didn't come around when the book was popular," said the woman. She shuffled away.

"It was never popular," muttered George. "And now, everywhere you go, sold out. Everywhere sold out."

They left. George grew moody. They stopped in a coffee shop and had some espresso. They stared at each other in silence.

"You're depressed?" said Jenny.

"Not at all."

"I'm glad. That's the most we haven't said to each other in a week."

George nodded appreciatively; he knew how rotten he was when he sulked, and he was grateful for her understanding. He stretched across the table and touched her hand.

"What are you thinking?" she asked.

"I think you're terrific."

"Maybe we should always keep quiet like this," she said softly.

•　　•　　•　　•

They sat in Avery Fisher Hall, Jenny transfixed by the Dutch pianist onstage, George surreptitiously cleaning his fingernails. George was deficient in music appreciation; he knew this, but could do nothing to correct it. He felt the guilt of the intellectual unable to savor an entire area of human culture. Frequently, he bought records—Schubert, Berlioz, Sibelius—and forced himself to listen for hours before giving up. He was too unrelaxed for classical music, too jittery, inattentive. He found rock songs jarring, folk music simplistic and monotonous, show tunes mostly banal. He wished it were otherwise.

"He's incredible, isn't he?" Jenny whispered.

"Yah," said George. He tried to stifle a yawn, but it forced its way out. He saw Jenny looking at him.

"Are you bored?" she asked.

"No, not at all."

"You *are* bored."

"No, no. I love it, I really do. He's excellent."

Jenny paused. "Well, I've had enough," she said finally.

"Good!" said George quickly. "Let's go." He grabbed her hand, and they flew up the aisle.

As they retreated through the many-tiered, glass-enclosed lobby, Jenny asked, "What's happened to me? I suddenly can't stand anything cultural."

"Schneideritis, perhaps," said George. "You get it from close association with a boor."

"Oh, you're not a boor."

"There is one other possibility," said George. "It tends to divert people's attention, makes for lack of concentration."

"What's that?" They approached the street-level exits.

"Infatuation," said George. "Causes stupidity."

They emerged into the luxuriantly lit plaza. The air was crisp, and Jenny pulled her coat tightly around her body. "Where are we going?" she asked.

"My place," said George.

"To do what, may I ask?" said Jenny with exaggerated stiffness.

"The Knicks are playing the Lakers," said George.

"You said it wasn't on TV."

George grinned. "Who said we have to watch?"

● ● ● ●

He fumbled a moment with the lock and key before the door opened. Taking her hand, he led her into the darkened living room without turning on the light.

"I can't see," said Jenny. "Aren't you—"

He pulled her close to him and kissed her deeply on the lips. Her mouth was soft and wet and acquiescent; after a moment, he felt her tongue gently exploring between his teeth. He intertwined it with his own, then slowly pulled away.

"Oh, God," she said, her eyes still not accommodated to the darkness. "I hope that was you, George."

"You'll never know," he cackled. He leaned forward and kissed her again. Once again, he forced himself to let go. "Okay, lady, this is a stickup."

"Everything I have is yours," breathed Jenny. She wanted very much to continue the kissing.

"I'm a mouth breather," said George, feeling

112

the need to explain. "My nose is just for cosmetic purposes. I think the inside is a coin bank." He flicked a switch and the lights went on.

Jenny shielded her eyes. "Ah . . ." she said. "At last, the vault of the beast."

"I prefer, 'The house that Schneider built,'" said George. "Less accurate, more elegant."

"Ohh . . . it's very nice, George."

"Of course. What did you imagine?"

"Mmm, more of a fraternity setting, I guess. You know, empty beer cans strewn all over, Farah Fawcett posters on the walls, springs popping from the couches, that sort of thing."

"That's the way it was this morning," said George.

"Actually," said Jenny, "I thought it would look exactly like this."

"Always glad to meet expectations," said George. "You want to take the tour?"

"What time does it leave?"

"You can just catch the last one," said George. He helped her off with her coat, and led her through the living room. "This is the living room," he announced.

"The *only* living room?"

"Well, there are thirty-six more," said George, "but this is the only one open to the public." He placed his hands on her shoulders as he steered her forward. "And this is the hallway that leads to the bedroom."

"The last mile."

"Or fraction thereof. Note the luxurious, though ostentatious, carpeting that lies on the floor of the house that Kenneth Hyphen built."

Jenny tilted her head up and back. "I want to see everything."

"Shall we start with the bedroom?" said George.

"Okay."

"If we start with the bedroom, we may end with the bedroom."

"Fine."

"You've no objections?"

"None at all. I enjoy touring in depth."

"Even tours that start at the end?"

"Endings are just beginnings backwards," said Jenny.

George bowed ceremoniously. "Ah, so. A fortune cookie romance, yes?"

"Yes."

They entered his bedroom, and immediately he kissed her. It had been a curious ten days. Except for light, affectionate good-night pecks on the cheek, they'd avoided virtually all physical contact. It seemed to be an understood, nonverbal agreement: Sex meant being serious; it wouldn't happen until they were ready for an extended commitment. Of course, it was an old-fashioned attitude, not so much a moral conviction as a matter of custom and comfort for people of their age. Each of them was aware of the artificiality of it, and yet, somehow, it had seemed the proper way to behave. The *right* way. And now their relationship was about to enter a new phase.

Jenny lifted her dress above her head, tossed it on the floor, and stood there in her slip. George inhaled sharply. She was even more beautiful than he'd imagined, and he'd fantasized considerably.

114

"Would you, uh, you know . . . like to use the bathroom, or something?" he asked.

"No," she said, "unless *you'd* be more comfortable." She grinned, and stepped nonchalantly out of the slip, leaving herself in panties and bra.

"I'm, uh, fine," croaked George. He sat on the edge of the bed, watching her.

"You don't look fine," said Jenny.

"I'm not fine."

"Is there something I can do to help?" said Jenny. "Maybe you'd feel better if you took off some of *your* clothes. I mean, it won't seem so silly if *both* of us are naked."

"Oh," said George. "Sure. Definitely." He removed his shirt and loosened his belt. "Look, there's something I should tell you."

Jenny stared at him anxiously.

"No, no, it's nothing serious," said George. "I mean, this isn't where I reveal an old World War II shrapnel wound that's left me impotent . . . if that's what you were thinking." He hesitated. "Actually, it's just the opposite, in a sense."

She looked puzzled.

George removed his trousers and stood up. "I, uh, haven't been . . . with a woman . . . in some time."

"No problem," said Jenny. "You'll remember what to do. It comes back to you."

"What I meant was," said George, "it's probably going to come back a little too fast."

"Still no problem," she said, coming over and running her hand down his chest. "I haven't been with a man in quite a while either. Besides, if at first . . . success comes too fast . . . try, try again. An old proverb."

"One last, awkward crudity," said George, breathing rapidly now. "Forgive the silliness, but I'm a believer in planned parenthood."

"And I'm equipped with more safety devices than a nuclear power plant," said Jenny.

"Now I *know* I'm in trouble," said George.

She stepped into the circle of his arms and kissed him deeply. He ran his hands up the backs of her thighs and over the smooth nylon of her panties. He felt the points of her bra press deliciously into his chest. She had to help him undo the clasp.

•　　•　　•　　•

Within forty minutes, they had made love twice. The first experience, as expected, was too urgent, too quick, over too soon. The second try was better; if not quite one of the all-time top couplings for either of them, it was at least very, very good—relaxed, gradually accelerated, mutually tender. Afterward, lying in the bed, George said, with a Spanish accent, "Did the earth move for you, my darling?"

"I think so," said Jenny. "It was either that, or the downstairs neighbors banging on the ceiling with a broom handle."

"They're a little sensitive on the lower levels," said George. "They lose sleep every time I boil water." He cradled her in the darkened room, her warm body tight up against him. He could scarcely tell where his own flesh stopped and hers began.

"Do you realize it's only been ten days?" Jenny said.

"Really? It seems hard to believe."

"I feel like we're at least into our fifth year."

116

"Maybe we are," said George. "Have you checked the papers lately?"

"No, I mean it, George. It doesn't feel like a new relationship at all."

"It doesn't, does it?" said George contemplatively. "I've noticed that too."

"I feel like we're picking up in the middle somewhere," said Jenny. "Renewing something that started a long, long time ago."

"Very mystical," said George. "Reincarnated lovers?"

"Maybe."

"You believe in reincarnation?"

"Mmm. A little." She turned her head. "You?"

"A little."

"Who do you think we were?"

"I . . . was Aristotle," said George, "and you were an usherette at the Acropolis."

"Male chauvinist."

"You see it differently?" said George.

"I was Helen of Troy," said Jenny. "You were my chariot driver."

"You had a chariot?"

"A small one," said Jenny. "Very good mileage."

"Maybe you want to be Plato?" suggested George. "I'll let you, no problem. There was a lot of talk in those days."

"Forget it," said Jenny. "I want us to be Jenny and George."

A full moon emerged from behind the clouds; its light streamed into the room.

"You are the sweetest girl," said George. He leaned over and kissed her. But as their lips parted, Jenny felt his body suddenly stiffen.

117

"What is it, George?"

"Nothing."

"Tell me," she insisted. "What happened?"

"Nothing," he repeated. "It's okay." He sat up, and she with him.

She turned then and looked behind her. On the end table, bathed in ghostly lunar illumination, was a photo of a woman. She was young, in her early thirties perhaps, and she sat on a beach blanket, waving and smiling at the camera.

"It's all right," said Jenny.

"I'm sorry," said George. He stood up and put on a robe.

"Whatever you're feeling," said Jenny. "It's all right."

He crossed to the window. "I . . . keep trying," he said. "I keep trying to push Barbara out of my mind. I can't do it. I try, but I can't do it."

"I know."

"The thing is, I don't really want to. Because I'm afraid if I do . . . I'll lose her forever."

"I understand, and it's all right."

"It's not all right. It's not fair to you."

"It's okay," insisted Jenny.

"There isn't a day that goes by that I don't think about her," said George. "Not one."

"That's perfectly normal . . . ."

"Then along comes Jenny . . . and I can't get what I'm really feeling straight in my mind."

"It will come."

"I'm not so sure," said George.

"It's all happened very fast. You expect so much of yourself so soon." Jenny paused. "I've always believed . . . that people can love more than one person at one time. And I'm not talking group

118

sex. I mean, having different kinds of affection for different people . . . so that you can go on loving someone without giving someone else up."

George seemed not to hear. "Some nights," he said softly, "I wake up in a cold sweat, and I say to myself, I'm never going to see her again, and I hope to God it's just a dream." He turned from the window, walked across the room and went out the door.

Jenny sat uncertainly for a moment, unsure what she should do, not wanting to disturb him further, and yet not wanting to see him so agitated. She found her panties on the floor and then slipped into the shirt George had worn to the concert. She found him sitting in the living room, a glass of red wine in his hand.

"I'm sorry," he said again, when he saw her.

"No matter what you're feeling now, George," she said firmly, "I want you to know that I love you . . . and I don't expect any more than you're giving me."

"You'll grant me some time?" he asked anxiously.

She nodded.

"Stay with me?"

"Of course," she said.

"Just give me the chance to tell you how happy you make me feel."

She came to him, sat gently on his lap, and put her arms around his neck.

"Careful not to spill the wine," he said. "This came all the way from New York."

"South side of the vineyard, I'll bet," said Jenny. She loosened the glass from his hand, took a sip, then placed the glass on the coffee table. He could taste the wine on her lips when they kissed. "I'm not going anywhere," she said.

"Not dressed like this, you're not."

"You can't lose me," said Jenny. "I know a good thing when I see it."

"I suddenly felt sick in there," said George.

"No explanations are necessary." She straddled his thighs with her own, felt his rising excitement.

"I didn't know what it was," said George. "Turns out to be a mild case of ecstacy." He ran his hand up above her waist. "You know," he added, "suddenly this shirt has taken on an entirely new dimension. After tonight I was going to throw it out."

She squirmed deliciously under his touch. He rose and carried her with him. "We've been up long enough," he said, heading toward the bedroom.

"Wait!" she squealed. "You promised me you would give me some of your books tonight."

"They're six-ninety-five each."

"I don't have any cash on me," said Jenny, "but perhaps I can arrange alternate forms of payment."

"Later," said George. "We can talk business later."

8

The majority of the guys lived in the Bronx, and so the game was held in Crotona Park. Touch football, safest sporting activity there was.

Wrong.

Since George and Leo had begun playing, there had been an average of one injury each week. Jammed fingers were common, sprained ankles, wrists and knees not at all unusual. One fellow had stepped in a hole in the field and broken his leg. Two others had been mugged on their way out of the park.

The rules allowed blocking, but no tackling. Naturally, if you blocked someone hard enough, he fell down. This was considered acceptable. There were six men on a side. George usually played quarterback, mainly because he wasn't strong enough to block, or fast enough to run. Leo played on the line, occasionally went out for passes.

George stepped up behind the center and looked over the defense. There were three offensive linemen, a halfback, and a split end. The play called in the huddle was a "turn-in," a pass pattern in which a receiver runs downfield, fakes toward the boundary, then cuts toward the middle where he catches the ball. George put his hands between the center's legs.

"Hut, hut!"

He faded back with the ball, saw a confusing mass of running, straining bodies and, before he could get any further bearings, was knocked to the ground by two bulky men. Slowly, he stood up, flipped the ball down and brushed himself off. Back in the huddle, he glared at Leo. "They got this new play in football, Leo. It's called blocking."

"I held them out ten minutes," said Leo.

"I think they broke your watch when they ran over you," said George.

"Come on," said Leo. "You coulda written a novel back there."

"Hey, girls," said one of the other men, "you'll pull each other's hair out later. How about let's play the friggin' game?"

"Right," said George. "Meanwhile, Lipsky, your pass pattern resembled a man sleeping on a bus."

Lipsky looked skyward, but refrained from further comment.

"All right," said George. "We need six big ones, and we need 'em *now!* Let's have Iannone and Lipsky split wide. You two cross about fifteen yards downfield, I'll hit whoever's open. Saul, you circle out underneath in case I have to go short. Okay? Everyone got it?"

There were no objections.

"Count of three," said George.

They broke the huddle and lined up.

"Ready?" said George. He checked the ends to

see if they were behind the line of scrimmage. "Hut-hut-hut!" The ball was snapped, and he faded back. Again there was a confusing jumble of bodies. This time three men came pouring in on him. He went down heavily, his elbow banging into his hip, the ball squirting upward. Lying there, he saw someone on the other team grab it in midair and begin to run.

• • • • •

They walked slowly along the concrete path, watching the curious game on the courts below.

"Puerto Rican handball," said Leo. "Five men on a side. They say it fosters a feeling of togetherness."

George grimaced. His body felt like one large sore. "You know the final totals?" he asked.

"Twenty-eight to nothing," said Leo. "But I think we'll have a psychological edge next time. I think we got 'em overconfident."

George shook his head. "You mad at me, Leo? Is that why you hired those guys to kill me?"

"One pass!" said Leo. "One goddamn pass you throw me all day."

"You want passes, tour the Sierra Madres."

"I'm blocking my ass off up there," said Leo, "and you're getting all the glory." He quickened his pace, then turned. "Go screw yourself, George!" He stalked on ahead.

It was an effort for George to catch up, but he pushed himself to move faster. "Hey! Leo! What's wrong?"

Leo shook his head.

"Hey, come on, I was just teasing. Hey."

Leo looked away.

"That's what big brothers are for," said George. "Here . . . you wanna gimme a nuggie?" He lowered his head.

Leo put his hand on George's shoulder. "Marilyn is leaving me."

George raised his eyebrows. "Are you serious?"

"What is that, a joke? My wife wants to leave me."

George shook his head. "Come, we'll take a walk."

They ended up at the Bronx Zoo, aimlessly traipsing through the grounds.

"But you still haven't told me why," said George, as they bent over the fence of the sea lion pool.

"She's got a list," said Leo. "Ask her, she'll show it to you."

"I don't understand," said George. "Exactly what is it that she resents?"

"She doesn't like my life-style," said Leo. "She doesn't like the hours I keep, my business, my friends, my indifference, my attitude, my coldness, and our marriage. Otherwise, we're in good shape."

A seal slithered out of the water and flopped up on one of the rocky outcroppings that protruded from the pool. He moved his head slowly to and fro, his sleek black body glistening in the sun.

"I said to her," continued Leo, " 'Marilyn, show me a press agent who comes home at six o'clock, and I'll show you a man who can't get Jimmy Carter's name in the papers.' "

"And what did she say to that?" asked George.

"She called me a stupid shit," said Leo.

The seal closed its eyes, appeared to doze.

"She's not going to leave you," said George flatly.

"She is."

"Leo, this has been going on for years."

"Not this time. She's leaving me the morning after 'Pinocchio.'"

"What?"

"Tina is doing 'Pinocchio' at school. Marilyn doesn't want to upset her until it's over. The kid isn't even playing the lead. She's only one of the herrings that get swallowed by the whale.

A second seal crawled up and lay motionless on the rocks.

"When is the show?" asked George.

"Thursday night. The only chance for my marriage is if it runs four years." Leo looked out over the water, then whirled around. "Listen, I don't know about you, but I didn't pay admission here to see two animals sleep in the sun. I want to see that, I can stay home and watch my neighbors." They headed off toward the monkey house.

Behind the first glass enclosure was a pair of mandrills, African baboons whose most spectacular features were iridescent blue ridges on both sides of their red-bridged noses.

"I should've brought Bambi here," commented George. "Give her some new makeup ideas."

Leo stared intently at the boxed-in, illuminated simulation of a jungle environment. "How'd you like to exist in there?" he asked vacantly. "I mean, spend your *life* in there?"

George shrugged. "Well, it is a little cleaner

than my apartment, I'll grant you that. The decor is a bit ripe, however . . . . I guess it would finally come down to the rent. If the—"

"That's what marriage is like, George."

"What? Marriage is two monkeys? I'm sorry, Leo, you were always deep, but this time your symbolism—"

"It's relentless. Every morning when you wake up, it's still there. You're still trapped, caged."

"It doesn't have to be," said George, moving on along the wooden railing. The next enclosure held a lone proboscis monkey. "Forgive the platitude, but it can be whatever you make it."

Leo shook his head. "I think maybe that's where you're wrong. I think, no matter who you are, or what you were, eventually the marriage makes you. It shapes you, controls you, restricts you to *its* boundaries." They began to move more rapidly through the dim hall.

"You're just down now," said George. "You had an argument, you're depressed, you see everything in a certain way. Just give it time."

"Time is just the point," said Leo. "Time is exactly what I need." He clutched George's sleeve. "If I could just get a leave of absence every once in a while. A two-week leave of absence. I used to get them all the time in the army, and I always came back."

"Women do not embrace such concepts," said George. "Not women of our generation, anyway. They may read about them, and even agree with them intellectually, but permitting their actual husbands to get outside R-and-R—never." They passed some squirrel monkeys, and then went out into the bright sunshine.

"The only note of optimism in all of this," said Leo, "is that in another thirty, thirty-five years, it'll be all over, right?"

"*Now*, you're talking heavy," said George. "Now, you're *really* talking restricted boundaries. Stick with this, and the both of us will end up on the subway tracks. Let's change the subject."

"You want to see the elephants?" asked Leo. "I remember years ago when we brought Tina, and we all watched one of the elephants take a gigantic crap right in the middle of the cage. She turns to me and says, 'Daddy, how come he makes doody in his living room?' I cracked up. I couldn't even give her an answer."

"We'll skip the elephants," declared George. "One may shit and bring on a two-hour binge of nostalgia. I opt for the reptile house."

"You would," said Leo.

They walked back past the seal pool, and then down a twisting, tree-lined cobblestone path that led to a cluster of low brick buildings. "Sure you don't want to see the great apes first?" Leo asked.

"The reptiles," insisted George.

They stood in a line that filed slowly past a series of glass cages. Motionless anacondas, pythons and cobras lay coiled in stagnant pools of water in re-created jungle tableaux. "I can't imagine why you find this interesting," said Leo. "To me, it's as entertaining as staring at the insides of closets. At least the monkeys move."

"The snakes have a kind of latent, pent-up intensity," said George. "It's like they're waiting for the right time to strike, not frittering away their energy."

"I think they're just lazy, dozing, good-for-nothings," said Leo. "You see how two people can interpret things differently? There's no such thing as objectivity."

They proceeded to a large tank that held three torpid alligators. A steel fence separated the tank from the spectators. Several people tossed pennies into the motionless water, a few of the coins striking the amphibians. "You're an interesting man, Leo," said George. "Someday, I'll have to get to know you."

"Take your time, no rush. You've got at least till the end of Pinocchio."

"Good. Because in the meantime, there's this terrific girl that I met ..."

"Who?"

"Jenny."

"You've gone out with her?"

"You sound like that's in a class with my jumping into the pool and trying to eat one of the alligators," said George. "Yes, I've gone out with her."

"And ... ?"

"And *what*?"

"You like her?"

"Yeah, I like her," said George. They came to yet another glass enclosure. A desert scene served as backdrop for a sleeping gila monster. "I *more* than like her, Leo."

"That's wonderful," said Leo with guarded enthusiasm. "I spoke to her for only two minutes, but I saw she had a vitality, a sparkle about her . . . I knew she would interest you."

"She more than interests me, Leo."

Leo seemed not to hear. "You want to see the House of Birds next?"

"I said, she more than interests me."

Leo, who had been ahead in the moving line, stopped and turned. "Good. I'm glad. I really am."

"I'm crazy about her, Leo."

Leo nodded. "Listen, I don't blame you. If I wasn't married, I'd have beaten you to the punch. Really, I think it's terrific. Want to catch the polar bears? They're right nearby."

"I'm in love with her, Leo. I mean *crazy* in love."

For an instant, Leo seemed stunned. "Love?"

George nodded.

"That's something."

They pushed their way outside. Straight ahead were the Great Apes, to the left were the Smaller Mammals; in the distance, the World of Darkness building loomed above the trees.

"Your choice," said George.

"Apes," said Leo, and they began to walk. "As far as 'love,' we'll see. The point is, you enjoy being with her, and at this time of your life, that's very important."

Two apes were being fed out of doors on a stone platform separated from the large crowd by a huge moat. One of the apes, a massive male, reclined against the wall of the building, nibbling from a nearby pile of leaves and vegetables. The other bounded around the platform, screeching and mugging at the people.

"I think he resembles you," said Leo to George.

"Yes," agreed George pleasantly. "A bit more muscular in certain areas, but our general demeanors are certainly similar." He paused. "If you're waiting for me to say that the other one acts like you— forget it. In the first place, he has better taste in food."

"And probably in women as well," said Leo. "Say, I wonder if we could sneak him onto our football team. He'd certainly improve the pass blocking."

George turned to face him. "I'm going to marry her, Leo."

His brother nodded absently. "Look, it's possible. I hope so. She seems very sweet, very bright. She could be wonderful for you."

"Leo, you don't understand, I *am* getting married. It's arranged."

"Terrific," said Leo. "Really terrific." He craned his neck to see over a man in front of him. The active gorilla was pounding on his chest, while his more relaxed companion continued nonchalant munching. "You know, I think the one in front is Jewish," said Leo.

"Why's that?"

"You see the way he's beating his breast? The *goyem* are more reserved. They hold everything inside, get nervous breakdowns."

"Leo, we're getting married on Monday."

Leo nodded. "When things calm down, when you get to be yourself again, I would love to see it happen. I really would."

George gripped his shoulder. "You have a hearing problem, maybe? We've taken the blood tests already. We have the license. Unless one of us has syph or clap or some other social disease—that's it!"

"Let's go see the giraffes," said Leo. "As long as we're talking about sticking our necks out. You know how long it's been since I've seen a giraffe in person?" He turned and started away from the crowd.

"You don't want to hear, do you?" George called after him. "Well, that's too bad, brother. 10:00 A.M., Criminal Courts building, Monday. Justice of the Peace."

Leo kept walking.

●　　●　　●　　●

On the subway going back home, they simply avoided the subject. Their car was filled with black and Puerto Rican teenagers. "Ever have the feeling you're out of place?" whispered George.

"Soon's I leave my house," said Leo.

One of the teenagers wrote "Off The Whites!" on the wall facing George.

"I think he's protesting the dress codes at certain tennis clubs," said Leo. "Frankly, I agree with him."

"If we live through this trip," said George, "I'm going to synagogue on Saturday, and I'm going to thank God with all my heart. Otherwise, He won't hear from me."

"We'll live, we'll live," said Leo. "These are good kids. Worst they'll do is puncture a lung."

They rode past three stations in nervous silence. Then, at 149th Street, a uniformed patrolman boarded the train and took up a position near the center doors. "Hold me back," said George to Leo. "I have this uncontrollable desire to run over and lick the tops of his shoes."

"Careful," said Leo. "I don't think cops care for perverts, even scared, grateful, whimpering ones. Besides, you'll have to wait until I finish polishing his nightstick."

Thirty minutes later, they walked through the

131

front door of George's apartment. Leo had started in again on the way up. "Twelve seconds! How can you marry a girl I spoke to in a theater lobby for twelve seconds?"

"Would it be better if she'd sung to you for five minutes? Or if it had been in a bowling alley instead of a theater?"

"At least I'd know if the girl could bowl," said Leo. He followed George into the bedroom.

"I'm not marrying a *girl*, I'm—"

"Your other choices are limited, Georgie."

"I'm marrying Jenny. Jenny MacLaine."

"Oh, good. You know both names. I guess you've spoken to her longer than I did."

George sat down on the bed. "I've lived with her for twenty hours a day for the last two weeks."

"Good! Congratulations. Another few months, maybe you'll get to know her."

"I know everything I need to know right now."

"Oh, sure. Certainly," said Leo. He paced irritably back and forth. "After all, you've been with her two weeks." He paused, then snorted contemptuously. "Two weeks. I eat eggs that are *boiled* for two weeks."

"So why blame me if you have the culinary discrimination of a goat?"

" 'Two weeks,' " mimicked Leo. "What the hell is that? That's nothing. Around here, it takes that long to find a parking space."

George removed his shirt and started unlacing his sneakers. "What happened to 'how interesting she is'? What happened to 'her vitality, her sparkle'?"

"Can't you wait to see if she still sparkles in six months?"

132

"Six days, six months, what the hell difference does it make?"

"Maybe all the difference in the world," said Leo. "Maybe a lifetime of difference." He dodged the sneaker that George lofted at him. "You know, your feet stink. Did anyone ever tell you that?"

"I never promised you a rose garden," said George. "I always thought that was one of those things even your best friend wouldn't tell you."

"I'm your brother, not your friend," Leo said. "I look out for you *better* than a friend, and it's exactly the point that I'll tell you what they won't. And my advice now is beware of whirlwind courtships. Winds have a habit of changing."

George stripped off his pants. "Jesus, what the hell are you, a human fortune cookie? You should get yourself a turban and a little shop on Eighth Avenue and go into business. The fact is, I knew Barbara for only eight weeks before we entered a marriage that lasted twelve years." He stepped out of his shorts and headed for the bathroom.

"I've wolfed down hamburgers in two minutes that've given me heartburn for days," said Leo, following him.

"I don't see the relevance," said George.

"The relevance is that it's not how long something lasts, it's the quality of the experience." Leo cupped his hand to his forehead. "Forgive me, my own life serves as a negative example."

"Leo, let's not get maudlin," said George. He stepped into the shower stall and shut the translucent door behind him. He turned on the water and adjusted the jets to a steady, stinging stream.

Leo loomed near the enclosure and raised his arm. "Hey, Georgie, remember the movie *Psycho?*"

George began soaping his body. "Remember the subway ride we just took?" He smiled. He loved it when Leo acted juvenile; it brought back memories of his childhood, confirmed that the world had still failed to squeeze all the little-boy playfulness out of him.

"George, you're vulnerable now. You're in no shape to make a decision like this. In fact, from what I saw before you got in that shower, you're in no shape to even walk from one room to another."

"Leo, you know me. I'm not self-destructive. I wouldn't do something to hurt me *and* Jenny just to satisfy a whim."

"Whims are not that easy to spot, and sometimes they're pretty powerful," said Leo. "In high school, I often had to satisfy my whims two, three times a day. You sure you're not confusing what you got with something like that."

George massaged shampoo into his scalp, felt mounds of warm lather rise in his hand. "Believe me, I'm old enough to distinguish love from sexual infatuation."

"It's not a matter of age . . ."

"I *love* Jenny. I want to be with her. I want to make this commitment."

Leo urinated into the toilet bowl. "It's all my fault."

"Not *all*, Leo. That's a bit grandiose, isn't it?"

"I mean, I never should've introduced you to Bambi. After Bambi, you were ready for anything." Leo flushed, and a few seconds later George yelped in pain. "What?" shouted Leo. "What happened?"

"The water," moaned George, frantically adjusting the faucets. "When you flush, it gets scalding. There's enough cold water for either the toilet or the shower, but not both. The management didn't figure this room for a two-person operation."

"Sorry," said Leo. "You okay?"

"Yeah, yeah, no problem. But I'll tell you, be a long time before I eat my next lobster. Poor little guys." George washed the shampoo out of his hair. "I don't know," he said after a while. "Maybe it *is* crazy. You always thought I was a little nuts anyway. It's just that I'm miserable every minute I'm away from her, and she feels the same way."

"You asked?"

"As a matter of fact, yeah."

"And you've evaluated this with your head, as well as your heart and your balls?"

George shut off the water and stepped out of the shower stall. "I think marrying her is a Class A idea, Leo."

Leo threw him a towel. "Okay, but what is she, Cinderella? She's leaving at twelve o'clock?"

"She's not going anywhere."

"So, wait! What's the rush? You'd wait six weeks for a dentist appointment, and that's with pain in your mouth."

George began to pat himself dry. "Every day we wait is a day we could have spent as man and wife. It's time lost."

"So spend it as yin and yang, or sperm and egg. I mean, what the hell's the difference what you call it, as long as you're together?"

George flicked the towel at his brother, who was too intent to even flinch. "Have dinner with us tonight, Leo. Check her out. Bring Marilyn along."

Leo reclined on the toilet. "I don't think a couple breaking up is the best company for a couple starting out."

"Let Jenny and me worry about that. What do you say?"

"I say, wait a month for me, George. Wait a month for me."

"I'm not marrying *you*." George reached for a yellow terry cloth robe that hung on a wall hook.

"Wait a month for me, and I'll wait a month for you."

"Huh?" said George, wrinkling his forehead. "You studying Zen, or something? Or are those song lyrics to some Scottish classic?"

"I'll try to work things out with Marilyn," said Leo. "I'll keep us together somehow for a month, if you and Jenny will do the same for me."

"Leo," said George, "we're not trading baseball cards now." He headed into the living room. "This is my life, that's your marriage."

"Exactly," said Leo, hurrying after him. "And I'm going to try to salvage it for both our sakes."

George faced his brother. "Leo, save it for you and Marilyn. Not for me." He turned and walked toward the bedroom.

"Why can't Jenny move in with you?"

"That's not the point—"

"Is she against that? She's not a Mormon or anything, is she?" Leo pushed open the bedroom door.

"I think she once saw Donny and Marie on TV, but that's as close as she got," said George. He plugged in the hair dryer and looked in the mirror.

"George, please, I can't talk over the din."

"Then talk under it." George felt the heated stream of air caressing his neck and scalp.

"Those machines are no good for you," said

136

Leo. "Did you know that? I read somewhere they lead to baldness."

"I'd rather be well-groomed now, even if it means being bald later," said George. "Or vice versa."

"I still didn't get your answer on the moving-in question."

George made a final flourish with the dryer, then shut it off. "We're wasting a lot of time, Leo. This conversation just used up my entire engagement period." He walked past Leo into the living room.

"All I'm saying is, deal with the past before you start something new," Leo called.

George didn't answer.

Leo emerged from the bedroom. "Make sure Barbara doesn't get in between you and Jenny."

"You're getting me crazy already, Leo."

Leo held up his palm. "You're right, you're right. I know, I'm entirely out of line. If it was anyone else but you, I'd just smile, offer congratulations, and walk away. But you . . . . Please—sleep on it. Take twelve Valiums, wake up in a month."

George chewed on his lip, then nodded slowly. "She'll wait if I ask her."

"Ask her."

"She'll move in if I ask her."

"Ask her. Please, George, ask her."

George crossed to the front door and opened it. He knew that if he spent another five minutes with Leo, he'd end up choking him. "Monday morning, Criminal Courts Building. I'm wearing a blue suit."

"Would you mind if I talked to her?" said Leo.

"For what purpose?"

137

"To tell her how I feel about all this."

"Yeah," said George angrily, "you're damned right, I'd mind. She doesn't need an interview to get into this family."

Leo dropped his gaze to the floor. He shrugged. "You're absolutely sure of this?"

"I'm sure."

Leo moved toward the door. "I hope so." He tapped George playfully in the stomach as he passed.

"Don't worry so much," said George. "Things resolve themselves without your help."

"I don't know what the hell I'm doing in publicity," said Leo from the hall. "I was born to be a Jewish mother."

George waved and shut the door. A moment later he was on the phone with Jenny.

"Hello?" said Jenny.

"I love you."

"Is this an obscene phone call? You'll have to speak up, if you want me to be really shocked."

"Do you love me?"

"Of course I do," said Jenny. "Who is this?"

George sighed. "I just told Leo about us. He thinks we're crazy."

"That's why they have brothers." Jenny grabbed a towel from the sink. She'd been cleaning the oven, and her hands were covered with grease.

"Jenny, I've been thinking . . . . Let's wait a month."

"Fine."

"Maybe even a couple of months."

Jenny paused, but made certain to keep the concern out of her voice. "All right, whatever you say."

"And I'd like you to move in here with me."

"I was right," said Jenny. "It *is* an obscene phone call."

"Just until we decide what to do."

"I'll move in whenever you want. Is six o'clock okay? There's some stuff I have to pack."

"I'm crazy about you," said George fervently.

"I feel the same way."

"Then forget what I said."

"You don't want me to move in?"

"I want you to move in permanently. Forever. Just show up on Monday exactly as we planned."

"I'll be there with my little bouquet," said Jenny.

They each made juicy kissing sounds into the receiver. "See you, babe," said George, and he hung up.

"I hope," whispered Jenny.

9

They met in the third floor reading room of the New York Public Library.

George was there first, seated at a table, the only person without any books in front of him. Jenny appeared in the doorway, breathless and excited. She spotted George immediately and hurried toward him, carrying a large package. They embraced before she sat down.

"I feel like I'm in one of your spy novels," she said. "Why meet here?"

George looked around with theatrical furtiveness. "Never mind that," he said in a Peter Lorre voice. "Have you got the microfilm? If the answer is yes, wiggle your left ear."

"I can't," said Jenny.

George pretended to pound the table. "I knew it!" he whispered urgently. "I knew the plan was flawed!"

Jenny grinned condescendingly. "Are you done?"

"Yes," said George sheepishly. "And the answer to your original question is that I wanted to revisit the scene of our first encounter. For purely sentimental reasons."

"That's sweet," said Jenny. "Except I haven't been here for five years. Could it be you're confusing me with one of your other girl friends?"

"No chance," said George. "It *was* you on that phone in the downstairs lobby. Or, at least, it was your voice."

"Ah," said Jenny. "I see, I see. They should put a plaque up." She nudged the package gently away from her. "Well . . . who goes first?"

"You," said George. "I can see yours."

She lifted the package and placed it in his arms. "Happy . . . whatever."

"Oy," he said, grimacing. "Heavy. I'm surprised you didn't get a hernia on the way over. What is it, a car battery?"

"Lead apron," said Jenny. "For when you cook on a microwave oven."

A woman next to them turned and held a finger to her lips.

George began to tear off the wrapping paper. The noise, of course, was hideous.

"Please!" said the woman, who seemed to be in her fifties. "This is a library."

"Sorry," whispered George. He tried to continue the tearing more quietly. Finally, with the paper half removed, he said, "Don't tell me—"

"Your first two books," said Jenny. "Doubleday's had to order them from the publisher."

"I thought these were only available at certain archeological digging sites," said George. "Jesus, this is amazing. You had them bound? In leather?"

"I thought rubber might be a little too kinky," said Jenny.

"I'm . . . I'm speechless."

"They're guaranteed to last as long as Dickens and Twain."

George held the books aloft. "I don't know what to say. I mean, the leather binding is beautiful, but . . . imagine it . . . I sold two more books . . . ." He leaned over and kissed her passionately on the lips.

"Please," she whispered. "This is a library."

"Just paying an overdue charge on my books," said George.

"Now mine," insisted Jenny.

George reached in his pocket, removed a small jewelry box, and handed it over. The woman next to them peered eagerly. "George, what have you done?" said Jenny.

"It's a car. Gets very good mileage."

Jenny carefully opened the box and withdrew a ring with a small diamond. "It's beautiful." She slipped it on her finger.

"Your basic wholesale engagement ring. The stone is flawless as viewed through the bottom of a sweet-cream bottle."

"Very nice," commented the woman next to them. "Myself, I prefer something a little larger, and the cut I like pear-shaped, but this is nice. It's the thought that counts, right?"

George smiled sourly before turning back to Jenny. "Last time I sit next to *her*," he whispered.

"Just one thing . . ." said Jenny.

"Don't say you don't like the cut—"

"No, no. It's just that we're only going to be engaged for two more days."

"I got this from a wino in an alley on Canal Street," said George. "What I paid, two days is all it'll last."

Jenny glanced around. "Let's go someplace where we can thank each other properly," she said softly.

George nodded, and they stood up. He put his arm around her.

"You can thank him right here," offered the woman in the next seat. "As long as you do it quietly."

"I don't think we can," said George.

•   •   •   •

Jenny was experiencing sensory deprivation. Her goggles, half filled with water, prevented her from seeing. Her earplugs prevented her from hearing, and her noseclip aborted her sense of smell. She moved clumsily in the indoor pool, knowing she was screwing up her kick by too much bending at the knee. She lifted her head way out of the water in erratic attempts at breathing. Flustered, she forgot to keep her fingers close together. After what seemed like minutes, she finally reached the far end of the pool and surfaced next to Faye's dangling feet.

"Tell you," said Faye, "for a pretty girl, you look like some klutz in the water. Is what you do called swimming or wallowing?"

"Wait," panted Jenny, removing the earplugs. "I just have to finish gasping." She inhaled and exhaled several times in quick succession.

"You certainly are equipped," said Faye. "I mean, just on gear alone, you should be able to cross the Atlantic. But I see it doesn't help much."

Jenny removed the goggles. "They leak," she said. "Problem is, if I make them tight enough to stop the water, they compress my head to the size of a plum."

"Their main function, then, is to hold the chlorine against your eyes," said Faye.

"That's about it," said Jenny. She looked up. "Wise guy. At least, I'm in the water."

"The really *good* swimmers all have webbed feet," said Faye. "I'm afraid I have some bad news for you, Jenny . . . . You stink."

Jenny removed her noseclip. "How'd you like this around your throat?"

"Seriously," said Faye, "why do you torture yourself?"

"Why? Because I have exactly two more days to get in shape. I'll never make it." Jenny paused. "How about you, aren't you coming in?"

"What for?" said Faye glumly. "I'm married."

Jenny pulled herself up out of the pool and sat down on the edge beside her. "You sound terrible," she said. "Is anything wrong?"

Faye pursed her lips. "We're not going away for the holidays."

"Oh, I'm sorry to hear that."

"Sidney's ear infection still hasn't cleared up. He's lost his sense of balance. He keeps rolling away from me in bed."

Jenny wiped her face with a towel. "I detect a note of bitterness there."

"Note? Try a concerto."

145

"Come on, Faye. You can't tell me things are worse at home than they are on the soap."

"The only difference between the two is that at home the sponsor doesn't break in every five minutes with a commercial message. Sometimes, I wish he did."

"Boy," said Jenny, "you really *are* down. I didn't realize . . . ."

Faye turned to her suddenly, her face showing the strain she was under. "If I ask you a favor, would you promise not to ask any questions?"

"Yes."

"How long are you going to keep your apartment?"

"My lease is up in two months," said Jenny suspiciously. "Why?"

Faye swallowed and said, "Would you lend me the key?"

Jenny, her mind whirling with the implications of Faye's request, focused her gaze on the diving board. "I have to get dressed."

"Jenny . . ."

Jenny stood up and started for the dressing room.

"Jenny, did you hear me?" Faye rose and followed.

"No. No, I didn't. Must be the earplugs. I think they leak even more than the goggles."

Faye put an arm on Jenny's shoulder. "Jen, this is important to me."

"Why do you want the key?"

Faye looked away. "You promised no questions."

"That's before I knew the favor." Jenny walked ⌐f the poolside benches and sat down.

146

Faye moved next to her. "All you have to do is say yes. There are worse things in life, kid. Some friends ask for money."

Jenny looked at her. "If you want the key, Faye, you can have it."

"But you don't approve . . . ."

"It's hardly my place to pass judgment. All I can urge is that if you're about to do something stupid—don't."

"Then forget the key," said Faye, "because I don't know a smart way to have an affair."

"Ohh, Christ! What have you done?"

"Nothing yet. That's why I need the key."

"I don't want to know who it is."

"It's a secret I'll keep to my grave."

"Jesus . . ." said Jenny, shaking her head. "The thing is, I know Sidney. I *have* known him for years . . . and I just feel—"

"Like you're betraying him," said Faye flatly.

"Yes."

"I can understand that. Think of the way I must feel."

"I'm trying, Faye. I am trying."

"All right, then. Let's call it what it is. I *am* betraying him. But, in a certain sense, *he* has deserted me. You can live with a person, you know, and even be sexually faithful to them and yet, in a more profound way, can nevertheless have abandoned them."

"Is that what's happened? Is that why you're doing this?"

Faye shrugged. "It's not important why. Really, it isn't. It's only important that I do it. And as for you, you are not being disloyal to anyone. Your involvement extends only to lending a key to a friend."

147

"Please," Jenny said. "At least, let me do my own rationalization."

Faye gripped her arm. "Don't you understand? If I don't have an affair, I'll scream."

"Then scream."

"Well, I figured I'd try this first."

"Have you thought about taking up jogging? Or tennis? Or bowling? *Anything*? Any other outlet?"

"The only outlet I think about is between my legs," said Faye. "And that's where my mind is most of the time. I'll admit, it's a nonintellectual pursuit."

They fell silent then, each somewhat embarrassed. "Well," sighed Jenny finally, "you're a grown-up lady. I guess you know what you're doing."

"The hell I do," said Faye.

"Is it mundane of me to point out you're not making any sense?"

"What does?"

"There *are* some options in the world that are more logical than others," said Jenny. "It's a matter of sitting down and thinking things through to a conclusion."

"*This* from someone who wears leaky goggles?"

"Everyone is entitled to one eccentricity. Besides, that's rather a minor peculiarity, no?"

"Okay. Then why are you engaged to a man you've known less than two weeks, a man who was married to a woman he idolized for twelve years? *Minor* me that!"

"Well," sputtered Jenny, "because, because—"

"Because yesterday was lousy, and it seems

___v."

"You're oversimplifying. Our situations are not—"

"I'll worry about tomorrow the day after," said Faye.

Jenny raised her eyebrows. " 'The Wit and Wisdom of Women in Trouble.' " She stood up. "Come on. I'll get you the key and a map of all quick exits from the apartment."

Faye patted her on the shoulder as they moved toward the dressing room.

• • • •

George dialed the number carefully, since it was a long-distance call. The phone rang six times before it was picked up at the other end.

"Hellaw?"

"Ma?"

"Hellaw?"

"Ma, this is your son, George Schneider."

"Who is this?"

"It's George, Ma. Your son."

There was a pause. "Oh, George. You know, for a minute I didn't recognize your voice."

"How are you, Ma?"

"I'm glad to hear you, George. I miss you, you know. I miss you like crazy. I think about you constantly."

"But otherwise you're okay?"

"Yeah, yeah, okay. What should I say? Usual pains and aches. Arthritis. Bursitis. Colitis. The old story. There's been some trouble in the condominium lately."

"Really? What happened?" George's mother lived in a development north of Fort Lauderdale.

149

"Well, two weeks ago, they found a piece of S-H-I-T in the pool. So, no one thought anything of it, the maintenance men cleaned it out, and it was business as usual. Except, the next day, it happened again. A day later, same thing, except more of it. A day after that there were ten, maybe eleven, pieces. Well, by the time they clean it, and filter the pool, half the day is gone. And who wants to go in after such a thing? It discourages you. So, anyway—"

"Ma—"

"At first, we thought maybe it's some little kid, a visiting relative of someone who lives in the condominium. But then, this past week, it was up to twenty pieces. Now—"

"Ma, I just—"

"—no little kid makes twenty pieces. So we figured, could be several kids, a group possibly. But what kind—"

"Ma, I'm getting married!" shouted George.

"What?"

"I'm getting married, Ma. Monday."

"You're getting married? To who?"

"I met a wonderful girl, Ma. She's adorable. You'll love her. I'll bring her down this winter."

"Tell her she might not be able to use the pool."

"I'll tell her, Ma. I'm sure it won't matter. She wants to meet you, and I know you'll like her."

"She Jewish?"

"Uh . . . well . . . no."

"I don't like her. " There was a moment's silence. "Of course, what you do is up to you. You're over twenty-one, you know what's best for yourself. I've always respected your judgment."

"Thanks, Ma, I appreciate that."

"Your judgment would've been better, of course, if you'd selected someone of your own religion but . . . I guess it wasn't meant to be. As long as you're happy, that's the main thing. My feelings are unimportant."

"They *are* important, Ma."

"No."

"Sure they are."

"I'll live, that's all. You think I'm one of these mothers who threatens to kill herself just because her son is marrying someone not to her taste? Believe me, I'm too smart for that."

"I know you are, Ma. But you'll change your opinion when you meet Jenny. I'm sure of it."

"Jenny, her name is?"

"Yes."

George's mother chuckled. "Well, at least she's not black, huh?" She paused, and her voice grew suddenly serious. "She *isn't* black. . . ."

"Oh, Ma. . ."

"Is she? With you, I don't know."

"She isn't. Just a little dark."

"What!"

"Just kidding, Ma."

"I know that. Whadda you think, after all these years your mother lost her sense of humor?"

"No chance," said George.

"Tell me, she comes from a nice family?"

"I suppose."

"You haven't met them?"

"No. They live in Cleveland."

"Cleveland, *nuch?* They have a house there?"

"Yes, I think so."

"How are they furnished?"

This was a standard early question whenever

151

George mentioned a new acquaintance to his mother. George and Leo often joked that if one of them mentioned they'd met Joseph Stalin, their mother would've immediately inquired about his decor. "I don't know, Ma," said George now. "I've never seen their place."

"He works, the father?"

"I think he's retired, Ma."

"What did he do?"

"Something in machining, I think Jenny said. I forget exactly."

"All right, you don't want to tell me, it's not important. You don't tell me anything anyway."

"Ma, please—"

"I'll speak to Leo, I'll find out. You've seen Leo lately?"

"Sure. We play ball all the time. Matter of fact, Jenny and I are visiting him later today."

"He knows about this, this romance of yours?"

"Ma, it's not a romance. We're getting *married*. And yes, Leo knows."

"Mmm. Well, all right. You should have only happiness and *nachas*. I wish you the very best for yourself."

"Thanks, Ma. You too."

"She works, the girl?"

"Jenny?"

"Yeah . . ."

"She's an actress."

"Mmm, well . . . okay. She's in the movies?"

"She's done some TV."

"She's taller than you?"

"No, I don't think so. Maybe an inch when she wears heels."

"Tell her to wear flats. Doesn't look nice when a

woman is taller than a man. I always wore flats when I walked next to your father, heshouldrestinpeace. You'll tell her?"

"I'll tell her, Ma."

"And remember, let her know she may not be able to use the pool when you visit."

"I will. I don't think that's important to her, Ma."

"Maybe instead of you coming down, I'll come up."

"Good. Fine."

"If you want me, of course."

"You're welcome anytime, Ma."

"You know I'm interested only in your happiness. Maybe I'll come in December. Crazy, huh? To come from Florida in the winter?"

"You were always unconventional, Ma."

"Yeah. Don't patronize your mother. I know more than you think." There was a pause. "I love you, George. I wish you and your bride the best, only the best."

"I love you too, Ma. Thanks."

He hung up. As usual after these conversations, he felt completely drained.

•   •   •   •

Leo's house was set on two acres of land just south of Rye, New York. It had five bedrooms, a full basement, a living room, den, study, and three full bathrooms. There were three color TVs, two separate stereo systems, two Cadillacs and an Oldsmobile in the huge circular driveway. A gardener came once a week to work on the lawn and sculpt the variety of unusual shrubs, and a cleaning woman was there Mondays and Thursdays to scour the house.

"It's all meaningless," said Marilyn Schneider, as she and Jenny unfolded a metal table on the patio. Marilyn was a serious, stiff-haired brunette who belonged to a variety of community service groups.

"I don't understand," said Jenny, who had just commented on the loveliness of the grounds.

"I mean, you can have everything and still have nothing," said Marilyn.

Jenny smiled nervously and looked around for George. She spotted him on the lawn, playing some kind of running game with the children, Bucky and Tina. Marilyn made Jenny uncomfortable; she was one of those women who wore her unhappiness on her sleeve, who would spill awful personal secrets to strangers. Jenny wanted no part of it.

"So," said Marilyn, "I hear you're an actress."

"Yes, that's right."

"You still intend to keep acting after you're married?"

"Sure," said Jenny. "I just may not travel as much, but I don't think I could ever give it up. It's my work. It's what I do best."

"Smart," said Marilyn glumly. "Always rely on yourself, always take care of yourself. As soon as you become dependent on someone—boom!—you're a prisoner. You become a slave to a certain life-style, and a part of you goes dead inside."

Jenny did not like hearing about dead inner parts. "Should I get a table cloth?" she asked.

"Pain in the ass," said Marilyn. She leaned closer. "Last week the gardener was, you know, a little

154

bit drunk, I think. Ran into the redwood table with the riding mower, knocked a leg off."

"The gardener?"

"The table. A carpenter was supposed to come yesterday, but, of course—you know these tradespeople—he never showed."

"Chairs," said Jenny. "We need chairs."

"I majored in Political History," said Marilyn. "Barnard College. I was really quite good."

Jenny was frightened that Marilyn might start to cry.

"Got halfway through my thesis," continued Marilyn, "and then I married Leo." Her lower lip quivered slightly, and she turned away. "Maybe I'll finish it one day."

Jenny felt a hand on her arm; Leo had appeared from nowhere. "Have you seen the horse?" he asked.

"Huh?"

He looked at Marilyn. "Did you show her the horse?" To Jenny he said, "We have a horse. You gotta see the horse."

Jenny shrugged. Horses were no bargain, but they were preferable to Marilyn. "Okay," she said.

Leo pulled her toward the stable, which was about fifty yards behind the house. "You like horses?" he asked as they ambled over the damp grass.

"I don't know any," said Jenny.

"We've got the worst goddamn horse in the world. Eats up twenty dollars a day, won't let anybody ride him, and craps up the entire two acres."

"I rode a horse once," volunteered Jenny. "It was at a dude ranch. I went there for the weekend.

155

His name was Buttons, and his idea of a good time was to veer under low hanging branches by the side of the trail. I came fairly close to forfeiting my face."

"Our horse isn't mean," said Leo. "Just stupid. He has the IQ of a flatworm."

Jenny stopped. "Maybe it's a thrill I could miss. I feel guilty about not helping Marilyn."

"No, come on," insisted Leo. "Forget her. I wanted a few minutes to talk to you . . . alone."

Reluctantly, Jenny resumed walking. "Sounds serious."

"No, not at all. I just wanted to chat."

"So chat."

"I had a few things on my mind," said Leo. They had reached the stable, and he looked around before pushing open the rotting wooden door. "It's really beautiful up here, isn't it? I mean, when you're not here every day."

They entered the stable. A bedraggled, weary looking horse stood immobile inside a stall. Its watery eyes scarcely moved at their approach.

"What's his name?" asked Jenny.

"Who cares? You call him, he doesn't move."

"Too bad. He doesn't seem like much fun."

"It could have been worse," said Leo. "They could have asked me for an elephant."

Jenny turned to face him. "What's on your mind, Leo?"

"You want to feed him a carrot?"

"Not particularly."

Leo nodded and inhaled. He held out his palms. "Where do I begin?"

"Don't look at me," said Jenny.

"I don't want to put this crudely." Leo hesitated. "I suppose the foundation for my thoughts . . . the, uh, the structure for my desire to . . . to what . . . to delineate the, uh—What the hell am I saying? The structure to delineate, what is that?"

"You think George and I are going too fast," Jenny said flatly.

"Yes," said Leo with relief. "Thank you."

Jenny stared at him unblinkingly.

"Why can't *I* think that clearly?" said Leo.

"From your point of view, two weeks must seem very quick."

"From here it's greased lightning. Be that as it may—and I hasten to add I never use expressions like 'be that as it may,' or even 'hasten to add'—I simply wanted to broach to you directly my concerns. If I seem, uh, unusually awkward, it's because this is virgin territory—well, let's say, not exactly virgin, but delicate, delicate territory—and I'm dealing with someone I care about very much."

"That makes two of us," said Jenny quietly.

"Good," said Leo. "I'm glad to hear it."

"What is it you're afraid will happen, Leo?"

Leo kept his eyes on the horse. "I used to do some P.R. work for an insurance company. They published a report that the greatest loss to a man or woman was the death of a husband or wife. Not even the loss of a child was considered as devastating, a fact I found pretty remarkable." He turned suddenly to face Jenny. "In time, most people work through it, Jenny. But it needs the time. And I wouldn't want you and George to be hurt because that time was denied to him . . . and you."

Jenny lowered her gaze. "I see," she said softly.

"What I'm trying to say is, please consider waiting for a while. Maybe it's best to get the past over with before you both start something new." Leo paused. "Is it unfair of me to ask that?"

"I don't know," said Jenny.

"Is it unreasonable?"

"It's not unreasonable . . ."

"But . . . ?"

"But maybe it's your timing that's throwing me a little."

"I'm sorry if I'm blunt."

"It's not the bluntness."

"It comes from twenty years in the newspaper business. I don't know any other way to be."

"I understand your concern for your brother," said Jenny. "I was hoping you'd have the same for your sister-in-law."

"Look, if I upset you, Jenny—"

She rolled her eyes upward. "God, how naive I am! I thought we were coming in here for you to tell me how happy George was."

"He is hap—"

"I thought I was going to get your blessing, not a warning."

"It's not a warning. It's a discussion," said Leo.

"Fine. We've discussed. I've seen the horse. Let's go back."

"Jenny, please. We're two intelligent adults here! Isn't there some—"

Jenny moved away from him. "I'm sorry, but just let me get angry a second, because I think I deserve it."

Leo cupped a hand to his forehead. "Believe me, I don't want to hurt you. I never would have brought it up—"

"I can only cope with one thing at a time, Leo.

158

Let me experience my happiness before I start dealing with the tragedies." Jenny remembered her discussion with Faye. Hadn't Faye expressed something similar? And wasn't it Jenny who had advised "thinking things through to a conclusion"?

"Happiness is all I wish you," said Leo.

"You know," said Jenny, "just getting married is a scary enough proposition, and I'm goddamned petrified."

"Why?"

"Because he loved her. Because he was devastated when she died. Because I'm moving into the woman's house Monday afternoon."

"That's my point," said Leo.

Jenny's lips tightened. "I *told* George I'd wait as long as he wanted."

"Yes, he said you would."

"Two weeks, two months, I don't care how long it is. But"—she extended an index finger—"it was *his* choice. He picked the date. If he feels he's ready to start living his life again, I feel very fortunate I'm the one he wants to live it with." She lowered her voice. "Do you understand that, Leo?"

Their eyes met. "I'm beginning to," Leo said.

"I'm the one who's gambling here," said Jenny quietly. "Not you."

"I agree . . ."

"And I'll tell you this, Leo. Even if what we're doing is not right, I'll *make* it right."

Slowly, Leo nodded. "Okay . . . I'll buy that." He went to Jenny and took her hand.

Suddenly there was a sound at the door. "Lunch is ready!" announced a high-pitched, childish voice. It was Tina, riding on George's shoulders.

159

"Who wants corn?" said George. "Speak up, 'cause we have to plant it right away."

Leo and Jenny moved away from the stall. "What *is* the horse's name, anyway?" Jenny asked.

"Sebastian," said Leo.

Jenny shrugged. "No wonder he's not right."

10

Ornstein, of course, ate with chopsticks. People who ate with chopsticks were always slightly annoying, as were people who wore wrist bands when playing tennis, or chef's hats when barbecuing. Some people, thought George, had to have all the accoutrements of an activity, no matter how fleeting or shallow their participation. He watched Ornstein attack a small piece of steak, and with a delicate pincer movement of his chopsticks transfer it to his mouth.

"I have trouble doing that with a fork," said George.

"Some people just have natural talent," said Ornstein.

They were in the Japanese Gardens, a restaurant on Fiftieth Street. Actually, Ornstein's eating reminded George of a giant prehistoric bird seizing a rodent in its razorlike talons, but he was not about to point this out. Ornstein, a trained psychologist, would no doubt find some deeply pathological meaning in the symbolism and shift it somehow onto George.

George squirmed in his seat. "You realize," he said, "this is the first time I ever saw you eat?"

"That right?" said Ornstein. "I don't keep track of those things." He dipped a shrimp delicately into a small bowl of ginger sauce before popping it into his mouth.

George saw Ornstein only occasionally now, at times of great stress or uncertainty. Their relationship, after so many years of twice-a-week analysis, was almost that of friend to friend, rather than doctor to patient. Of course, Ornstein knew George too well—and the knowledge was all one-sided—for them ever to be *really* friends, but a social afternoon or evening was something each of them could enjoy.

"It's nice to know analysts perform human bodily functions," George said, watching Ornstein chew shrimp.

"Only on Sundays," said Ornstein. He poured himself some saki. "Want some?"

George shook his head no.

"Tea?" Ornstein also poured himself some tea.

"No. Thanks."

"Advice?"

George chuckled. "I miss our sessions. If nothing else, you were always good for a laugh."

"At my price, you gotta give them *some*thing," said Ornstein.

It was true. Ornstein had always been entertaining. He was blunt and earthy. Sometimes he'd listen to a convoluted rationalization of George's that would last thirty minutes and then say, "You're full of shit," and George would have to grin. Ornstein could talk and listen on any subject: the Knicks, auto transmissions, castrating mothers, vacations in Greece, anxiety attacks, paddle ball—*any-*

thing!—for fifty dollars an hour. "A bargain," he'd say, and then explain for the hundredth or two-hundredth time how and why George was a failure in interpersonal relationships and what could be done about it. "So," he said now, "what's new?"

"Not much," said George. "I'm getting married tomorrow morning."

Ornstein nodded. "Can I have the sugar, please?"

George passed the sugar. "Refined sugar is the worst thing in the world for you," he said.

Ornstein smiled. "Getting married . . . . Well, that's really nice. Congratulations. How long have you known her?"

"Two weeks," mumbled George, quickly shoveling some steak into his mouth.

"How long?"

George held up a palm to indicate a pause for chewing. "Two weeks," he repeated.

"I can understand why you mumbled," said Ornstein. "How did your friends react to this?"

"They suggested I see a shrink. Or at least have lunch with one."

"You have smart friends," said Ornstein.

"Sometimes."

"How do *you* feel about it?"

"I made the reservation, didn't I?"

"Why? To get them off your back? To get some kind of official sanction? Or what?"

"I don't really know," said George. "I guess just to talk to someone who knows me better than a lot of my friends. And relatives. I can't seem to analyze my own feelings."

Ornstein looked disgusted. "Do you love the girl?"

"I'm crazy about her," said George. "I know that she makes me happy. I just don't know how Barbara's going to feel about it."

Ornstein rolled his eyes. "Barbara's dead."

"That's easy for *you* to say."

"Don't you believe it?"

"Yeah. I was at the funeral. Then again, maybe it was all one big joke, some kind of elaborate trick, a hoax. Barbara could walk through the door right now, sit down at the next table, and it wouldn't surprise me."

"What would you say to her?"

George shrugged, "Oh, something cool . . . like, 'Hiya, hon. Nobody called.'"

Ornstein chuckled appreciatively.

A white-aproned waiter approached and asked if everything was all right. "Fine," said Ornstein. "My compliments."

Earlier, the waiter, a hulking Japanese, had put on a display of whirling swordsmanship, using several wicked-looking knives and cleavers to hack and dice the steak and peel the shrimp, which were then cooked on the spot. The effect had been theatrical and a bit frightening.

"You know," said George, when the man had backed away, "as a finale, at the end of the meal, he returns and beheads a few of the customers."

Ornstein pursed his lips. "Well, if I'm one of the chosen, he can just forget his tip, I'll tell you that." He looked piercingly at George. "Which reminds me—what have you been dreaming about lately?"

"Look, if you want me to lie down, the wooden bench is too hard," said George.

Ornstein shrugged. "You're paying for the lunch. I just thought I'd ask."

Ornstein, George knew, was a champion dream analyst. At the beginning of his therapy, George had never remembered his dreams, but as the sessions wore on, he found himself able to recall isolated images, then sequences, finally entire plots complete with dialogue and scenery. And though often the dreams on a given night seemed completely unconnected—one might be about herrings, another about truck driving, and a third about intercourse with drowning victims—Ornstein could always unearth a brilliant thread that linked them together, showed them as merely different aspects of the same obsession or neurosis.

"It's pretty much the same scene," said George now. "I'm with Barbara at a party on the beach. Suddenly, for some reason, she gets angry with me and walks out. She's furious. I try to get her to come back, but she pulls away. 'Leave me alone,' she yells. 'Just leave me alone.' She goes off with someone else—it's twilight, dusk, and I can't see his face. Anyway . . . I'm desperate. Panic-stricken. I plead with her not to be angry with me. Her face . . . I never saw that look before." George exhaled. "After that, I usually wake up. I can't get back to sleep, I feel so alone. It's so real, so vivid . . . I feel helpless, frustrated. I want to talk to her, but she seems just out of reach." He paused. "Lately I'm afraid to go to bed, because I can't face another night of someone hating me that much."

Ornstein raised his eyebrows, but otherwise remained expressionless. "So . . . what does it all mean?"

"*I* should tell you? Gimme fifty bucks, and you'll get an explanation. Who's the expert here?"

Now Ornstein smiled. "On your dreams, it's

you. It's as if you were a geologist, and I were a local guide. I can take you to the abandoned mine, but you're the one who has to analyze the ore. You want a place to start, I'd suggest the anger."

"But that's just it," said George. "I don't *know* why she's angry. I haven't given her any reason."

"You haven't?"

"No."

"You don't call leaving her forever a reason?"

"But, but I— She left *me!*" sputtered George. "*She's* the one who left!"

"And you're angry with her."

"No! Not angry, I'm—"

Ornstein nodded. "Hurt. And, yes—angry. Of course. Don't apologize. You have a right. The subconscious mind is very primitive, see? Like an animal. All it knows is that it's been abandoned. It's not too wonderful at analyzing causes. It's been deserted, so it gets angry."

"But in the dream, it's Barbara who's angry . . . ."

"Well, maybe a little projection is going on there," Ornstein suggested. "After all, it's not too acceptable being angry at a dead person, especially a dead person whom you loved. So the mind turns it around. Listen, kid, it ain't easy for a nonverbal being to express grief. You gotta look and listen very hard—or else it'll keep trying forever."

"It's a pain in the ass," said George.

Ornstein concentrated on his plate. "Why is it so important to get married tomorrow?" he asked. His voice had the forced casualness that always signaled a major question.

George breathed deeply. The problem was . . . he did not have a major answer. He felt a pressure

166

building now, as if, unless his response was satisfactory, the marriage would somehow have to be canceled—a victim of internal logic, dissolved by psychoanalytic decree. Ornstein had once explained to George his expectations concerning the course of treatment: *You*, a writer, should theoretically be the best of all subjects, he'd said. After all, the writer's stock-in-trade was verbalization of the emotions, bridging the gap between conscious and subconscious, recognizing and exploiting symbolism. For you, I have high standards, Ornstein had pronounced. George had always felt inadequate, not smart enough; it was as if Ornstein had formulated the rules of therapy to favor George, then easily beat him at his own game. He had even told Ornstein this, exposing his own feelings of inferiority, and Ornstein had promptly denied it. "I can only analyze," he'd said. "*You* can synthesize, which is a far more difficult task. Besides," he'd added, "who says it's a competition?"

Now, George felt the tension build as he groped for an answer but came up with nothing. He wanted Jenny . . . because he wanted her. He supplied his own rebuttal: *Repetition does not constitute explanation.* "Because when I wake up in the middle of the night," he blurted angrily, "Jenny is there." He waited for Ornstein's disapproval, waited for the superior analytical intelligence to expose his emotional shortcomings, his bankrupt ideas, his ultimate shallowness and pedestrian intellect.

He was surprised when Ornstein shrugged, pinched a shrimp expertly with his chopsticks, and said, "That's not a bad reason."

● ● ● ●

Monday, at 9:00 A.M., Leo's cab pulled up in front of George's building. Leo, neatly dressed in a blue pin-stripe suit with a carnation in the lapel, paused as he prepared to get out.

"I'll be down in five minutes."

Marilyn shrugged, pinched her lips together.

"You okay?"

"I'm fine," said Marilyn stiffly.

"Marilyn, we don't have to be civil to each other through their entire marriage. Just for the wedding, okay?" Leo slammed the cab door and headed toward the building.

Upstairs, in his apartment, George had just finished the surgical procedure that other men called shaving. He wore three separate pieces of toilet paper on his cheeks and chin, which, aided by the application of a styptic pencil, he hoped would stanch the bleeding. He had put on a shirt and tie when the phone rang.

"Hello?"

"George?"

"Hello, Ma. Ma, I can't talk to you, I'm leaving in two minutes."

"That's all right. I just remembered a few things I wanted to ask you about, uh, what-was-her-name . . . ."

"Jenny."

"Jenny."

"Ma, I already told you everything."

"What does her father do?"

"For a living?"

"Of course, for a living," said George's mother.

"He's something in machining. A machinist."

"And he works in Cleveland?"

"Yes," said George patiently. "He also lives there, that's why he works there." He saw his knuckles whiten as they gripped the receiver. "You'll meet them all when you come up from Florida." He heard a loud buzzer. "Hold it a second, Ma, the doorbell's ringing."

"My doorbell?"

"No, mine!"

He let the receiver dangle from its cord, shook his head, then rushed to the door and opened it. Leo brushed past him.

"I'll pay for your entire honeymoon if you take my wife with you," said Leo.

George shut the door.

"What's wrong with your face?" said Leo. "Is that a suicide attempt?"

"I cut myself shaving," said George. "I can't stop bleeding. Was there any royalty in our family?"

"Yeah. King Irving from White Plains." Leo paused. "Where's your shoes?"

George looked down at his feet, still clad in slippers. "I slept twelve minutes all night. And I woke up twice during the twelve minutes." He sat down, bent sharply forward, and probed with his hands under the couch. After a moment, he withdrew a pair of black loafers. "The Thom McCans," he announced. "I was hoping for the Buster Browns, but I guess it's not to be."

"Enough with the jokes," said Leo.

"Sometimes I get one Thom McCan, one Buster Brown. I figure that's a reasonable compromise." George put on the shoes.

"Come on, hurry," said Leo. "If you're late, this judge fines you."

George looked up. "Who is she, Leo? I'm marrying a girl, I don't even know who she is."

Leo extended an index finger. "Don't start in with me. You drove me and all your friends half crazy."

"In your case, it was a short drive, Leo."

"I don't care if she's a koala bear," said Leo menacingly, "you're getting married today. You're getting married if it kills you."

"Which reminds me," said George. "I can't breathe. I can't draw a deep breath."

"No? Then take two short ones."

"Seriously, what a day I pick not to be able to breathe. What should I do, Leo?"

"I'll buy you a balloon, you can suck on it."

"Now who's cracking the jokes, making wise-aleck remarks while his brother endures a major life-crisis."

"Please," said Leo, "don't give me a dramatic show here. If you're gonna call this off, let me know because I can still catch a workout at the gym."

George stood up, glaring. "Will you have a little compassion!" he yelled.

"Thanks, I already had some," said Leo.

"You think getting married is so easy? You think all you—"

"Who's on the phone?"

"What?"

"The phone. You left somebody hanging?"

George spotted the dangling receiver. "Oh, Jesus! It's Mom. Talk to her!"

Leo strode toward the phone as George began to open a flower box that had been delivered earlier. The flower was a carnation, fastened with what

170

seemed like three hundred staples to a piece of cellophane-covered cardboard.

"Mom?" said Leo into the phone.

"Hello?"

"How you doing, babe?"

"You sound hoarse, George. You have a cold, maybe?"

George wrestled with the flower, at first trying to unbend each staple, then gouging at the cellophane with his fingernails. "I think they packaged this to go on the space shuttle," he said.

"It's not a cold, it's Leo," said Leo into the phone.

"Who?"

"Leo, your son's brother."

"This isn't George?"

"No, Ma, this is the other one. Remember? You have two."

The cellophane was making wild crackling noises. George began to bite it. "Sonofabitch!" he said, driving a fist into the carnation. "I'll get this sucker if it's the last thing I do."

"Mom, we gotta go," said Leo. "I'll call you tonight." He hung up, then crossed to George. "What are you doing? What is that, a forest fire?"

"I'll ... kill ... this ... thing," said George, pounding futilely now at the flower. "Kill it!"

Leo gently moved it away. "Don't give up," he said. "The judges have you ahead in two rounds, the carnation leading in three, and one even. I think it'll tire as the fight goes on."

George looked up. "You were right, Leo. It's all too soon. I should have waited until eleven, eleven-thirty. Ten o'clock is too soon."

Leo had the flower half unwrapped. "Come on. I'll finish this in the cab."

"Why must you humiliate me on my wedding day?"

"It's no humiliation," said Leo. "Some people just happen to have hands like pliers, and others like loaves of bread. It's because of individuals like you that mankind was motivated to develop tools."

George grabbed his jacket, and they headed toward the door. "Wouldn't it be interesting," George speculated, "if man's rise to dominance was traced to a petrified carnation somewhere that some poor cave dweller couldn't take out of its package?"

"Let's not get stupid," said Leo.

"I didn't even have breakfast," said George, in the hall.

Leo shrugged. "I'll buy you an Egg McMuffin at McDonalds."

•   •   •   •

They sat for an hour in a green-painted, airless, partitioned city office, waiting for the Justice of the Peace to arrive.

"Judge, he be late today," explained one of the clerks as each new couple presented their marriage license.

The heat seemed to stifle conversation. George, Jenny, Leo, Marilyn, Faye—all sat stiffly, their eyes on the lone electric fan atop the chief clerk's desk. On a bench opposite them were eight colorfully dressed Puerto Ricans, whose ages and looks were so disparate that George found himself unable to guess which pair was getting married. A huge black man in a business suit walked in, arm-in-arm with a wispy shorts-and-halter clad blonde. An obese woman berated, in Yiddish, a slim, balding old man. In the aisle, a pair of perfect-looking, sun-browned teenagers stood alternately fondling each other and laughing.

"It was either get married or go to the beach," whispered Leo.

George stood up and walked to the clerk. "Any news yet on the judge?" he asked.

"Judge be soon," said the woman. "You gots to have patience. Judge, he a busy man."

George nodded and returned to his group.

"Well?" asked Jenny, squeezing her small bouquet.

"Judge, he a busy man," said George.

Ten minutes later, another clerk called "Schneider and MacLaine!" George and Jenny walked to a window. "Sign here, please," said the clerk, shoving forward a form. They wrote their names. "Witness?" said the clerk.

"We have two," said George. Leo had agreed to witness for George, and Faye for Jenny.

"Form only got space for one," the clerk intoned.

Leo deferred to Faye.

"Chapel is five dollars," the clerk added.

The chapel was a tiny room, bare except for a pulpit and an American flag. Leo, Faye, and Marilyn stood soberly while the judge, an aged black man, administered the marriage vows to Jenny and George. ". . . then by the power vested in me," he concluded, "I now pronounce you man and wife."

George and Jenny kissed. Faye bit her lip. Marilyn stared icily ahead, while Leo used a fingernail to remove a particularly annoying chunk of wax from his left ear.

On the way out of the building, Marilyn and Leo threw some rice at Jenny and George. "It was a choice between this and powdered potatoes," said Leo.

"Tell me," said George, on the steps outside. "Am I the only one who's crying?"

"The only thing I know," said Leo, "is that the judge had a bad eye. Did you see his eye? I think he married me and George."

Marilyn touched Jenny on the shoulder. "Have a wonderful trip, Jenny. I'm very happy for you."

"Thank you," said Jenny. "We'll all have dinner as soon as we get back." She kissed Marilyn on the cheek. "Thank you very much."

Leo handed George a large envelope. "All right, here are your plane tickets, your hotel reservations, and complete honeymoon instructions. Come out of your room at least once a week, food is very important."

"If, after six months, we emerge and see our shadows," said George, "I think that means a long winter. Either that, or a good year for my urologist." He paused, and met Leo's gaze. "Thank you for everything, Leo."

"For what?" The brothers embraced.

"Okay," said George, breaking away. "Let's go! Which one of you girls is Jenny?"

Jenny looked around, saw Faye hanging back on the steps. She went over and held out her hands. Faye took them in her own and forced a smile. "I'm sorry Sidney couldn't be here."

"I am too," said Jenny. They hugged each other then, both their faces wet with tears.

"I feel so damn silly," sniffled Faye.

"We're all silly," said Jenny. "That's what life is." She hesitated. "Whatever you decide to do, Faye, is all right with me."

Faye nodded, and wiped her eyes. "I have never been so envious of anyone in my entire life."

Jenny kissed her once more, then hurried back to George. "Good-bye," said George. "Good-bye. Say good-bye."

"Good-bye," repeated Jenny.

A taxi was waiting at the curb. "It's our honeymoon," George told the driver as he and Jenny got in. "Take us anywhere."

Slowly, the cab pulled away. Jenny leaned out the window, holding the bouquet. "Catch, somebody!" she yelled, and flung the wilting clump of flowers.

Without thinking, Leo snatched it out of the air.

11

The place was called Milbridge, Maine, and it was only fifty miles from Canada. The small, six-seater plane came in low over the crystal waters of Pleasant Bay and gently descended toward a long flat rectangle of green land that stretched almost to the shore.

"That's either the airport runway or somebody's bedspread," said George. He was relieved when they finally touched down. He had been positive their tiny craft would be hit by lightning; he had envisioned a tragic scene in which he and Jenny hugged while the plane corkscrewed into the Atlantic.

"Smell that air," he said, as they walked toward the small airport terminal.

Jenny inhaled deeply. "I can't take it," she said. "My lungs have adapted to a mixture of smog, carbon monoxide, and sulphur dioxide. What is this garbage I'm breathing?"

"It's called air," said George. "Clean, fresh, Maine air. Go on, keep inhaling."

"Tell me when to stop," said Jenny, "and catch me if I pass out."

Five minutes after entering the uncrowded terminal, Jenny and George had retrieved the three suitcases that constituted their luggage. A man wearing a blue cap approached them. "Mr. and Mrs. Schneider?"

"Yes," said George.

"Hi. I'm the chauffeur from Bayview Resort. The car is outside."

George turned to Jenny. "Told you it was a classy place."

They traveled for nearly forty minutes along a single lane road that took them past narrow crescent beaches, shining waters dotted with bobbing sailboats, lush forests, log cabin summer homes, and stark, granite-lined inlets.

"So, what do you think?" said George, holding hands with Jenny in the back seat.

"It's okay if you like perfection," she said.

"It's all fake, you know. The ocean. The trees. It's all rear-projection—for the tourists. The natives live in apartment houses."

Jenny leaned over and kissed him.

"Your first time at the hotel, sir?" asked the chauffeur.

"Uh, no," said George. "I've been here before."

"That right? How long ago was that?"

"About twelve years." George paused. "Have they changed it much?"

"We try not to," said the driver.

Jenny squeezed George's hand a little tighter.

• • • •

Bayview Resort had a large main building and a number of outlying cottages; George had opted

178

for one of these. Jenny was out on the terrace before he had finished tipping the bellhop. Through an opening in the trees she could see a huge crimson-and-apricot sun begin to quench itself slowly in the distant waters of the bay. She gasped as George came up behind her and enfolded her in his arms.

"Let's not go back to New York," she said. "Let's buy a little place up here. You can write your novels, and I'll become a lumberjack."

"Pancakes and maple syrup the rest of my life? I'll go nuts," said George. "And get fat, too. Nobody needs an obese crazy person."

"We can exercise . . ."

"Fine. You feel like running?"

"Now?"

"Yeah."

"Okay. Where to?"

"The bed," George said.

Jenny began to laugh, but it wasn't long before she stopped.

•   •   •   •

The next day, they took a tiny sailboat out on the bay. Jenny lay soaking up the sun, while George fiddled with a cassette tape recorder.

"You should take your shirt off," said Jenny, who wore a bathing suit. "Get yourself a tan."

George looked up. He was so clumsy with anything mechanical that he was having trouble getting the cassette into the recorder. "I already have a tan," he said. "I've been working at it. My skin is now pasty white, which is much darker than normal. Besides, everyone knows honeymooners aren't supposed to be sun worshippers."

Jenny stared at his shorts. "Too bad. You have a nice physique, you know. You really ought to show it off, especially your ass."

"You want me to show my ass?"

"It's beautiful."

"Well ... thanks. Yours, too. Still, I don't think I ought to display it publicly here in Maine. It's more a New York thing to do. I'll wait till we get back."

"Which reminds me, where'd a city boy like you learn to sail?"

"We had a big bathtub."

Jenny dipped her hand into the cool water. "I just can't resist jumping in."

"Go on," said George. "We'll take turns. I'll stand first watch."

Jenny got to her feet. "You promise you won't leave me?"

"How much life insurance did you say you had?"

"Five dollars."

"Have you made me the beneficiary yet?"

"Not yet."

"Well, then, there you go. You're safe. Besides, I'd have to eat dinner all alone, and you know how I hate that. Go on. Trust me."

"The last time I heard those words I wished I had a can of Mace," said Jenny.

"Just don't tip over the boat when you go in," said George. "The nearest I come to swimming is watching old Esther Williams movies."

Jenny plunged over the side, disappeared briefly, then splashed to the surface. "It's gorgeous!" she squealed. "Fantastic!"

George pressed once more and felt the cassette

click into place. He was pleased; after all, he'd been planning this since before the honeymoon. He hit the "Play" button, turned the volume up high, and the theme music from *Jaws* thundered out over the water.

George stood up. "Jenny!" he yelled, gesturing frantically. "What's that behind you?"

She turned and screamed, and her shrieks mingled with his laughter.

●　　●　　●　　●

There was dinner and dancing outdoors on the terrace of the main building. George sat back in his chair, unaware of the disco music, unaware of the couples on the floor, his gaze fixed on a cluster of distant stars.

"Hey!" Jenny broke in.

George blinked. "What?"

"What are you so quiet about?"

"I wasn't quiet. I was just listening to the wine fermenting in my stomach."

"Always the wise-aleck . . ."

George shrugged. "All right then, I was thinking."

"Oh," said Jenny. "Well, you think very quietly." She hesitated. "Is anything wrong?"

"No . . . ." said George. "I'm sorry. I don't know where I was." He stood up. "Come on, let's dance."

They did a rather genteel hustle, until George said, "I can either talk or do this, but not both. Unless you're interested in hearing, 'one, two *and* three,' over and over."

"It doesn't make for exciting conversation," said Jenny.

Ignoring the music, they switched to a fox-trot. "I never did figure out why it takes all my intellectual abilities and powers of concentration to do a dance teenage girls master effortlessly," said George. "I think anyone who can hustle ought to get a full scholarship to Princeton."

"The idea is not to think about it," said Jenny. "At least, so I'm told. The rhythm is supposed to be in your bones."

"Not mine," said George. "I believe mine is somewhere around the gallbladder, and I don't have to tell you how low-rated *that* organ is. Some people get it removed just because they don't like its name." He became aware of another couple dancing rather close to them.

"George?" said the man tentatively.

George looked puzzled.

"I thought it was you." The man smiled. "I'm Lee Michaels."

"Yes. Lee, how are you?" said George. He stopped dancing and shook the man's hand. Michaels was a short, balding fellow who perspired heavily.

Michaels turned to Jenny. "We had the cottage next to George and his wife. I think they were just married then." He giggled. "We used to get together every two, three years. Oh"—he clapped a hand to his forehead—"almost forgot. This is Gwen."

Gwen, a bony, cherry-redhead, smiled thinly.

"And this is my wife, Jenny," said George.

"Hello," said Jenny.

Michaels smiled unctuously. "Ah . . . very lovely. Very lovely indeed. Pleased to meet you."

"Same here," offered Jenny.

"We come back here every year," said Michaels. "We brought the kids this time." He indicated two boys eating ice cream at one of the tables. "They're having a ball."

"How old are they?" asked Jenny.

"Well, Jeffrey, the one nearest, is six. And Stuart, the one with chocolate all over his face, is seven."

"Stuart takes after his Dad," said Gwen.

"Very nice," said Jenny.

Michaels reached out and put a hand on George's shoulder. "Listen, uh, we were very sorry to hear about—"

"Barbara." George wondered vaguely how Michaels knew. Bad news seemed to be transmitted by telepathy.

"Barbara," echoed Michaels. "She was a lovely girl."

"Thank you."

"Gwen lost her sister about two months ago—"

"Cancer," interjected Gwen.

"—so we know what you must have, uh, well . . ."

"Yes," whispered George.

"Anyway," said Michaels, brightening, "you're looking good. Gonna be here a while?"

"A while," said George.

"We'll see you around." Michaels and Gwen resumed their dancing.

"Nice meeting you," called Jenny.

George led her back to the table. "I'm sorry," he said.

"For what?"

"For not thinking things out clearly."

Jenny shrugged.

On their way back to the cabin, on the winding

183

stone path, Jenny paused to examine the sky. The night was clear and moonless; swirling pinwheels of sparkling blue stars flung milky streamers to the limits of the jet black horizon.

"Gorgeous, isn't it?" Jenny took off her shoes. "I read somewhere that the light from some stars, the light we see now, started out millions of years ago. It's like looking into the past."

"Jenny . . . how do you feel about kids?" In the darkness, George's face was indecipherable.

"That's not an uninteresting question," said Jenny.

"And the answer?"

"I don't know."

"Have you ever thought about it?"

"A little. Not much. I don't think I was ready. I had enough to deal with just trying to make the marriage work."

George nodded. "Funny, before, when we met Michaels, I couldn't help feeling . . . I dunno . . . sad, sad for his kids. I know it's a terrible thing to say, but I kept picturing them growing up with sweaty palms and becoming accountants or something, and . . . well, it was just depressing."

"You feel that way about children in general?"

"No . . . I really don't know. Barbara was pregnant twice. . . ."

In the darkness it was easy for Jenny to hide her surprise. George had never mentioned this before.

"Lost them both in the fourth month," George continued. They began to walk again. "Maybe we were better off."

Back in the cottage, they had prolonged, satisfying sex before sinking into exhausted sleep. It was past 4:00 A.M. when Jenny stirred and extended an arm to pat George's neck. Feeling only pillow, she sat up and looked around the darkened room. "George?"

No answer.

She spotted a dim figure seated on the terrace. Quickly, she slipped on a robe and went outside. The air was still, not the slightest hint of a breeze; night creatures chirped and buzzed intermittently. "George? Are you all right?"

No answer.

"Couldn't you sleep?" She kissed the back of his neck, reached one hand around to stroke his forehead. He was perspiring.

George pulled away slightly at her touch. "I'm . . . uh . . . I'm sorry, Jen." He remained facing away from her.

"For what?"

"It was stupid to come back here . . . ."

"No—"

"I didn't think."

"It's all right, George. It really is."

He shook his head. "Christ, I think this was the same cottage. I can't even remember."

"We don't have to stay. There are other places." Her voice was pleading now.

"I've *been* to other places. It doesn't seem to make much difference."

And then, suddenly, she was angry. Grief was one thing, but this prolonged, excessive chasing after the dead, that was . . . unfair. "Then why *did* we come here?"

He shrugged. "You tell me."

"I wish I could. I wish I could crawl inside your head and somehow exorcise all the loneliness

185

and the bitterness, and leave only the sweet memories and some harmless nostalgia—but I can't. No one can. You have to deal with it yourself, come to terms, or block it out, something—or you may as well give up now, George, and go live in the past."

He snorted and shook his head. "The terrible thing is, I can't seem to remember her the way she really was. She was an incredible athlete. I couldn't keep up with her in the water, had to fight for my life on the tennis court ... but those are never the images I get when I try to think of her. All I see is this beautiful girl lying in a hospital bed wasting away to nothing. She—"

"Why must you torture yourself like this?" Jenny moaned. "Why?"

George seemed not to hear. "She was in such agonizing pain that I couldn't get close enough to even touch her. When I came to the hospital, I always had to knock on the door so she could fix her hair and try to get some color into her face. We'd talk about the weather—as if it could matter to her there—and our friends and politics, and never once, not a single time, did she cry in my presence. Right up to the last few days, she had her hair up in a ponytail and tied with a little blue ribbon."

Jenny felt the anger drain from her. She reached out and gently began to massage George's neck.

"We never once talked about her dying," he said softly. "The doctors kept telling me, 'two weeks now,' then 'one week at most,' and finally 'any time,' and yet—she lived, she fought. I think somehow she imagined she was going to get up and leave that place. That we'd go back to the beach that summer. That she'd run me off the tennis court again."

"George—"

His voice was an anguished whisper. "They called me in the middle of the night. She just slipped away . . . and I wasn't there for her."

"Please, honey—"

He was sobbing, and his body shook. "I never even said good-bye."

Jenny knelt in front of him and cradled his head in her arms. "It's all right, George. Shhh. . . . It's all right."

"I'm sorry . . ."

She kissed his forehead. "You feel cold as ice. Come back to bed."

He pulled himself up and wiped the tears with a corner of his robe. "I will, I will."

"Come . . ."

"Later. A little while. I promise."

She waited a moment, touched his face again, then rose and walked back inside.

George lingered a long while in the dark. "Oh, Leo . . ." he said quietly. "When the hell did you get so smart?"

•   •   •   •

She was up early the next morning, but not early enough. From the terrace, she saw him in the distance, walking alone on the beach. Once, he stopped for a moment and turned his face to the sun before continuing.

They ate a Continental breakfast in the main building. Other couples around them were talking animatedly, but George continued to sulk, saying little, and looking distracted. Jenny thumbed through a brochure as they finished their coffee.

187

"You know, it says in the winter here you can rent snowmobiles. I've never been on one. I'll bet it's a lot of fun."

"Mmm," said George.

"All right, what do you feel like doing today?"

"Anything . . . . Whatever you want."

"There's a golf course nearby. You play golf?"

"Not really."

"Okay . . . ." Jenny looked at the brochure again. "How about a bike ride?"

"Sure," said George indifferently.

"It says there are some beautiful old paths up through the mountains."

"Terrific." George's tone was icy.

"We don't have to if you don't want to."

"I *said* it's all right. You want it on paper, I'll write it out for you."

Jenny looked away, fighting back a rush of tears. A man whose dead wife had never cried during her illness would not appreciate a maudlin display of emotion. "I feel," she said shakily, "as though I've done something wrong, only I haven't quite figured out what it is yet."

"I'd like to go back today," snapped George.

Jenny nodded. "If that's what you want. . . ."

"We could rent a car and drive down to Boston. Get a shuttle flight. It'll be quicker." He exhaled. "Do you mind terribly?"

"I mind when I don't know what it is you're thinking about. I mind when I feel I'm on this honeymoon alone."

"Alone?" George chuckled mirthlessly. "No. The last thing we are is alone."

"I don't mind going back, George, I swear to

God. As long as I know that when we get home, we can start tomorrow fresh."

"Fine. We'll pack as soon as I finish my coffee."

"I just want to be included in this marriage," said Jenny. "I don't think I'm asking for too much when all I want is the chance to make the both of us happy."

"Then don't push me!" George said loudly.

People at other tables turned to stare, then quickly looked away.

"You don't have to yell," said Jenny.

"I'm not yelling."

"You are."

"All right, I am. So what. Don't try to force her out of my mind, because I need whatever part of her I can hold on to. I'm not ready yet, Jenny . . . ."

Jenny stood up. "I'm not going to stay here and have you holler at me."

"I'm not ready because I'm just not willing to give her up that easy."

"The entire dining room is watching us. Are you aware of that?" said Jenny.

"Fuck 'em," said George. He wiped his mouth with a napkin, threw it carelessly on the table, and rose. "I'll go tell the management we're checking out."

12

It was raining heavily when they got back to the apartment. George pushed open the door with one of the suitcases and reached inside to turn on the light. Dripping wet, he and Jenny trudged into the living room.

"Some downpour," said Jenny.

"The lightning," said George. "Did you see the lightning? It looked like an advertisement for the end of the world."

He dropped the large suitcases near the couch, while Jenny put her smaller bag on a chair. Her hair was plastered to her neck by the rain. She moved toward a window to check some potted plants. George examined the mail, opening envelopes one by one.

"Thirty-eight-dollar phone bill," he said. "Imagine if I actually used the instrument to talk."

"Your African Violet looks like it has sleeping sickness," said Jenny. "We better water it and give it some food."

"There're some hot dogs in the freezer," said George. "Maybe it would like them." He opened another envelope. "Look at this. A new book club specializing in ESP. They claim they foresaw I would join."

"Any mail there for me?" asked Jenny.

"You've only been living here thirty-eight seconds. Even the ESP book club isn't that fast."

Jenny frowned. "Is there anything soft to drink?"

George sat down on the couch. "I think there's some beer. I could strain it if you like."

"No thanks," said Jenny. "I believe we have all the strain we can handle." She went into the kitchen. There was no beer in the refrigerator, only an open bottle of Coke. She took it out and put it to her lips. "Want to share some soda?" she called.

"Nope."

She returned to the living room, carrying the bottle. "Sure? There's none of that annoying fizz to worry about."

George looked up. "I'm sure. What happened, it was open?"

"Mmm hmm."

"Too bad. Must've been the 'easy twist-off cap.' When I finally pried it loose—I mean, after the screwdriver, the pliers, and the acetylene cutting torch—I guess I was in no mood to stick it back on."

"Well, no moods are good moods," said Jenny, with a false, jolly brittleness. "Better than walking around with a chip on your shoulder."

George stared as she took another swig of the Coke. "How many glasses of wine did you have on the plane?"

"Two."

"How many?"

"Four."

"You had seven."

"I had six," Jenny said.

"And two at Logan Airport. That's eight."

"All right, it was eight."

"You had eight glasses of wine?"

"Right. Not seven. Don't accuse me of having seven."

George brought the two suitcases into the bedroom. "You're tight!" he shouted.

Jenny followed him. "Oh, is that what's been bothering you all day, George? That I drank too much?"

"It doesn't bother me, it's just not a good thing to do, that's all. If you're not used to it, it can make you sick."

"Oh, so now you're interested in my welfare."

"Though said sarcastically, that happens to be correct."

"Well, I can't help it, I don't like flying," said Jenny.

"Neither do I. It's something you put up with. What's the worst that can happen? Pain and death, that's all. It's not like the worries are anything serious."

"I asked you to hold my hand," pouted Jenny, "but you wouldn't do it. So I drank some wine instead."

George put a suitcase next to the bed. "I *did* hold your hand. And while I was holding it, you drank my wine." He brushed past her into the living room.

"I'm hungry," she said, trailing after him.

"So make something to eat."

"Unless you're fond of bread mold, there's nothing in the refrigerator. How about sending out for pizza?"

"I don't feel like pizza," said George.

"Then why don't we *go* out and get a chili burger?"

"Jenny, I'm tired."

"And out of sorts?"

"Tired. You want one, go yourself."

She came up behind him. "Oh, come on, George."

"I said ... no." He bent over to fluff the carpet where the suitcases had rested.

"A gorgeous ... fattening ... greasy ... dripping ... hot chili burger ...."

George said nothing. Jenny reached out and goosed him with the Coke bottle. He snapped upright, his face furious. "Cut it out, goddamnit!" he shouted.

Jenny took a step backward. She had misjudged his mood. This was more than cranky, little-boy sulkiness, or even melancholia; this was full-blown, aggravated hostility. "I'm sorry," she said, surprised but not cowed.

"How many times do I have to tell you, I don't want a goddamn chili hamburger?"

"Chili *burger*," corrected Jenny. "For someone who's a writer, you'd better learn the idiom of the commoners. The ham is silent, like Hyphen Hill."

"Oh, very good. Occupational attack, double entendres, all launched within seconds. Give the girl two gallons of wine and some uncarbonated Coke, and the repartee really gets quick."

"Never as quick as you, George. I'm just a dumb old country girl from Cleveland."

"Right. And Sam Ervin was just a poor country

lawyer. Don't put yourself down, Jenny. You can hit and hurt and badger with the best of them."

"I don't even know what that means," said Jenny. "I've spent the last two days trying to be understanding, bending over backwards, considering your every sensitivity—and you, you can't even find it within yourself to be civil. Is this how it's going to be? Do I have to think out everything I say two days in advance for fear it *may* touch on some sore point of yours?" She shook her head. "It's awfully hard to live like that, George."

George held up a palm. "Jenny, it was a long trip, I'm tired, you're tired, it's raining out—please don't push me."

"I don't see what the rain has to do with anything. And believe me, the last thing I want to do is push. My only concern"—her voice softened—"is trying to keep my husband happy. When he's blue, I am also."

"I'm not blue. I get that color only when I swim." He chewed his lower lip. "Listen, I'm walking a very fine line tonight. There are a lot of things I would like to say that would just get us both in trouble."

"Honesty will not get us in trouble. . . ."

George headed for the bathroom. "I don't want to deal with it now. Let's save the honesty for tomorrow and just be pleasantly deceitful tonight."

"I don't think that's much of a basis for either a relationship or a good night's sleep," said Jenny. She lingered outside the bathroom door while he opened the medicine cabinet.

"We'll sleep," said George. "Let's just go to bed and hope that two extra-strength Tylenol can do all they claim to. Okay?" He swallowed two pills.

"I'd just as soon hear what you had to say."

George squeezed a quarter-inch of toothpaste onto his toothbrush and began to scrub his teeth. "Ah duh thik you duh."

"What?"

"Ah duh thik you duh."

Jenny squinted at the blue bubbles on her husband's lips. "You know, at the rate you're going you'll get dishpan mouth. Rinse out, so I can understand you."

George rinsed out. "I don't think you do," he said finally.

"Why don't you let *me* be responsible for what I want to hear," countered Jenny.

George examined the inside of his mouth in the mirror. "All right. . . . As honeymoons go, I don't think you got much of a break."

"Really? I'm sorry you feel that way."

"And I'm sorry it turned out that way."

Jenny shrugged. "Shows you how much I know. I thought it was wonderful."

"Gums," said George.

"What?"

"Very important. Most mouth problems in older people are caused by gums, not teeth. Bet you weren't aware of that. And you know what's the first-line weapon in the war against gum disease?"

"Harmonicas," said Jenny. "Look, why are you trying to change the subject?"

"Floss," said George. "Smart people use dental floss every night." He shut the medicine cabinet door. "The trouble is, I don't have any." He walked past her back into the bedroom.

"I happened to have a wonderful time in

Maine," said Jenny. "And if you were grouchy for a couple of hours, well, that's hardly reason to complain. Which I never did. As far as what went on in the past, I think we ought to limit this conversation to present honeymoons."

"Why?"

"Because that's where we're living."

"You can't get to the present without going through the past."

"Jesus, George, is that what you did in Maine? Compare honeymoons?"

"Compare, no. There is no comparison." He hoisted a suitcase onto the bed and opened it.

"I have the feeling I just came off second best," said Jenny.

George removed a stack of shirts and placed them on the dresser. "Why don't you ever ask me questions, Jenny?"

"I don't understand. . . ."

He returned to the suitcase as she sat down on a corner of the bed. "Why do you treat our lives as though there never was a day that happened before we met?"

"Maybe I'm not overly curious."

"Don't give me that."

"Then maybe I'm trying to spare your feelings. Maybe that's my trouble, I look out too much for you and not enough for myself. If there are things you want to tell me, then tell me!"

"I will."

"Good. Fine. I'd be delighted to hear them. But for God's sake, does it have to be on our first night in this house?"

George reached into the suitcase and pulled out

197

his electric razor, a hairbrush, and a nail clipper. "Jesus, I was wondering when that perfectly calm exterior was going to crack."

"Oh, is that it?" said Jenny. "This has all been a game, then? See how much Jenny will take before she opens up? Well—yes, I've cracked."

"Good! Thank God for a little healthy antagonism."

"Antagonism, hell! That's pure fear. And there's nothing healthy about any of this. It's sickness. deep, lingering, festering sickness that I'm terribly afraid now will infect the both of us."

"Why?"

"I have terrific animal instincts. I know when my life is about to be threatened."

George waved derisively. "You're being melodramatic. As a writer, I recognize the form."

"If you're going to patronize me, George, I can't talk to you."

He threw several bunches of socks onto the dresser. "Aren't you even curious to know who we are?"

"I know a sufficient amount to have married you. Isn't that enough?"

"I wonder," said George. "Sometimes I think you've got some goddamn romantic image of this man with a tragic past, right out of *Jane Eyre*."

"You're the one with the writer's imagination," said Jenny sarcastically. "Not me. I'm merely melodramatic."

George turned, hands on hips. "All right," he challenged, "tell me about Gus."

Jenny's eyes widened briefly before she looked away. "What would you like to know?" she asked softly.

198

"Well, I mean, he's got to be more than just a comic figure in a football jersey."

"He was never comic."

"Fine! Then tell me something about him. What was your honeymoon like? Was he a good lover? Or was that something else he fumbled on the five yard line?"

Jenny wrinkled her face. "Clinical? You want clinical? You expect me to stand here and give you a detailed description of what it was like in bed with him?"

"Why not?"

"I don't believe that, George. I don't believe you actually want to hear how we did it, and how many times, and what positions, and whether he was bigger or smaller than you, and what sounds we made. *That* is not what you want."

"Why don't we just forget it," George snapped. He walked out of the bedroom.

Jenny remained seated. "Why are you doing this to me, George?" she said softly, quite aware that he couldn't hear. "I don't understand what it is you're after." There was a squeak as the door to the hall was opened. She ran into the living room just in time to see him leaving. "Where are you going?"

"Out."

"Where?"

"For a walk."

"But it's raining . . ."

George shrugged and kept moving.

"I'm coming." She closed the door behind her and followed him into the elevator. "Talk to me, George," she said. "Don't shut off."

George stared straight ahead.

"I get so lost when you shut me out. . . ." pleaded Jenny.

A massive fat woman got on at the fourth floor. She was carrying a plastic basket full of clothing. She looked back and forth from George to Jenny. "You don't know how glad I am you're here," she said.

Jenny forced a polite smile. She wondered if the woman meant her personally—perhaps she knew George—or whether it was simply the collective presence of reasonable-seeming people.

"Last week," said the woman, "I went down to do the wash, there's a Spic in the elevator. I get to the basement, he takes out his thing."

"Very nice," said George, striding out of the car as they reached the lobby.

"He's not concentrating," Jenny told the fat woman as she hurried after George. In the street, she said, "George, I will try anything that's going to make us move closer to each other."

"Good," said George, heading downtown on Central Park West. "I'll take out my thing."

"Please," said Jenny. "Be serious. Don't put up a barrier."

"I said forget it," he barked, speeding up his pace.

"*No,* goddamnit!" shouted Jenny. The rain had tapered off, leaving only a warm drizzle. "You're not going to open me up and walk away from it."

"I need a rest," said George. "You're not giving it to me."

"Damn right, I'm not," said Jenny loudly. A woman walking a poodle turned to stare. "I went through one marriage ignorant as hell. At least let me learn from this one."

200

"You'll learn some other day . . . ."

"Oh, no! No, sir. I'm not going to blow five years of analysis in one night because you haven't got the nerve to finish what you started."

In the distance, the green dome of the Hayden Planetarium shone dimly against the night sky. "I have an idea," said George. "Why not have your psychologist talk to my psychologist? That way the two of us needn't bother."

"I *want* to bother," said Jenny. "Believe me. You asked before why I never questioned you. Okay, let's begin the mutual inquisitions. Unwrap our sordid pasts. You show me yours, I'll show you mine. You want to go first?"

"You're doing fine on your own."

"All right . . . tell me about Barbara."

They headed into the little park on the north side of the Museum of Natural History. "We'll probably be mugged and killed in here," said George. "Or vice versa, if we're lucky."

"Fine," said Jenny.

They found a bench facing the planetarium. George wiped off the rain water before they sat down. "Our best chance," he said, "is if the criminals figure us for decoy cops. Try to look like a cop."

"Barbara—"

"She was terrific," said George.

"Oh, I know she was pretty," said Jenny. "I see enough pictures of her around the apartment."

"It *is* my apartment."

"*Our* apartment now."

"And any pictures *you* may elect to put up are certainly welcome."

"Tell me about your honeymoon," said Jenny. She wished she'd brought a sweater. The damp air

201

was beginning to give her a chill. "After Maine, you went to Europe, didn't you?"

"Paris, London, and Rome. Notre Dame, Champs Élysées, Buckingham Palace, Westminster Abbey, the Coliseum, the Fountains of Bernini—have I dropped enough names?" He lowered his voice to a savage whisper. "And if you want a romantic description, it was a knockout."

"So much for the big picture," said Jenny. "I got the adjectives, what about the details? Aren't you going to fill in those? Big room, or small? View overlooking the Seine? Four-poster bed? And what was the wallpaper like?"

George cupped both hands over his ears. "Stop it!" he shouted.

"Why? What's wrong?"

He shook his head.

"Would you rather make out a list? What's safe to talk about and what's hands-off?"

"Jesus," said George, "I don't have the strength for this kind of thing anymore."

"You were doing fine a few minutes ago."

"That was my last ounce of energy. I'm sorry, Jenny, I don't think I'm up to this tonight." He rose.

"Why, George? Why is it so painful? What are you feeling now?" She followed him up the stone path that led out of the little park.

"I'm feeling like a corned beef sandwich," he said suddenly. "You want? There's a delly on Seventy-fifth that stays open late."

"You wouldn't come with me for a chili burger . . . ." said Jenny.

"This is different. Corned beef stands to chili burgers as Mallomars do to Lorna Doones."

202

"That's profound," said Jenny. "All right, I'll come." They headed toward Columbus Avenue.

"I used to go sleigh riding in that park," said George. "My parents would bring me and Leo." He looked back. "Christ, that was so long ago, so long . . ."

Jenny took his hand. "I want to know something. Do you imagine that I'm expecting you to behave a certain way? That I want you to act as if this were your first marriage?"

"No," replied George. "*I* expect it. I expect a full commitment from myself. I have my own standards. I did it twelve years ago. . . ."

"But?"

He inhaled. "But I can't do it now."

"I'm in no hurry," said Jenny. "What you're giving me now is enough."

"Then you're too easily satisfied," said George.

"I'm patient," said Jenny. "I know the rest will come."

George stopped walking. "Really? How?"

"Well—"

"*How* do you know? How the hell did you become so wise and smart? Stop being so goddamn understanding, will you? It bores the crap out of me." He resumed his stride.

"Then what *do* you want?"

"I don't know."

"Bitterness? Anger? Fury? Is that how *Barbara* would have reacted?" The "Barbara" came out with a mocking, exaggerated scorn; Jenny wished she could pull it back. "Is that it? Do you want me to behave the way she did?"

"Here's the delly," said George, pointing.

"Well, I'm not Barbara!" shouted Jenny. "'And

203

I'll be damned if I'm going to re-create *her* life just to make *my* life with you work!"

"Control your ranting," said George quietly, as they entered a small kosher delicatessen. The place was virtually empty.

"How many?" asked an elderly waiter.

"Two," said George.

The waiter looked around at the sixteen unoccupied tables. "You're in luck," he said. "I think we can squeeze you in." He led them to a booth, where they sat down.

"I'll just have corned beef on rye, a tombstone, and a Dr. Brown's cream," said George. "Jen?"

"What's a tombstone?"

"A square knish."

Jenny nodded. "Same for me."

"Thank you," said the waiter. "Be right back."

Jenny leaned forward. "This is *our* life now, George. Yours and mine. I am not Barbara. The sooner we start accepting that, the sooner we can get on with this marriage."

George studied her carefully. "No, you're not Barbara. That's clear enough."

Jenny sipped water from the glass in front of her. She felt a large balloon slowly expand inside her chest and throat, fought against the relentless pressure it exerted, the sensation that it would burst through her skin and explode in a shower of blood-drenched viscera. "Oh, George," she managed to choke out. "If you want to hurt me, you don't have to work that hard."

"Sorry," said George, folding and unfolding his paper napkin. "But you give me so much room to be cruel, I don't know when to stop."

"I never realized that was a fault," said Jenny. Her water glass was almost three-quarters empty.

"Until now . . ."

"Yes," she said.

"I guess it's one of the minor little adjustments you have to make. But I have no worry. You'll make them."

"Corned beef!" announced the waiter musically. He slid plates with two meaty sandwiches in front of them. "I assume you wanted lean," he added. "If not, we saved the fat, we can give it to you as a side order."

"Lean is fine," said George. "How about the knishes?"

"Knishes and sodas coming," said the waiter. "Gotta bring them separate, they weigh too much." He chuckled. "Good thing you didn't order the stuffed derma. For that, we need a crane." He shuffled back to the counter.

"You resent me for adjusting?" asked Jenny. Looking at the food before her, she realized she had no appetite.

"I resent you for *everything!*"

"But why? Why is that?"

George tore a chunk out of his sandwich. "Because I don't feel like making you happy tonight. I don't feel like having a wonderful time." He glanced up as the waiter returned with the rest of their order.

"You don't want a good time, you came to the right place," joked the old man. "You should enjoy your meal anyway." He smiled and walked away.

"You know," said George, "I don't think I wanted a terrifically wonderful honeymoon. You're after happiness, Jenny? Then find yourself another football player, will you?"

The tears ran from Jenny's eyes. Her lower lip quivered uncontrollably, and she tried to cover her face with her hand so that George would not see.

"I resent everything you want out of a marriage that I've already had," he continued mercilessly.

"Stop . . ." she whispered.

"And for making me reach so deep inside to give it to you again. I resent being at 'L' or 'M' and having to go back to 'A.' And most of all, I resent not being able to say in front of you . . . that I miss Barbara so much." George, too, began to sob. He blew his nose into a napkin.

"This is ridiculous," said Jenny, her eyes red-rimmed.

"I know," said George.

"A waste of good corned beef."

"I know." He shook his head. "Oh, Christ, Jenny, I'm sorry . . ."

"It's my fault."

"I think I need a little outside assistance."

Jenny nodded. "What do you want to do?"

"We'll call the waiter. See if he'll get us a doggie bag for the sandwiches."

"I mean . . . about us."

"I know very well what you mean." George paused. "I don't know. I don't want to make any promise I can't keep."

"Up to you," said Jenny. She slid over to the edge of the booth and stood up. The anger and the tears were gone, replaced now by a single-minded coldness. She regarded George remotely, and when he reached out to take her hand, she deliberately drew away.

206

13

The stage door led to an alley off Lafayette Street; Jenny, high heels clicking on the pavement, reconnoitered briefly as she emerged from the alley, then started uptown. A shaggy-haired man in a gray sweater came running after her.

"Jen! Wait—"

Jenny kept walking. The man held a thin booklet under his arm. "Hey! Wait a second!" She stopped as he drew close.

"Martin, I'm sorry," she said.

"What's wrong?" said Martin. "Hey, come on. It's not the first time someone's run out of an audition." He took her arm. "Come on, I got the script right here."

Jenny shook free. "I can't."

"Yeah, yeah. That's what they all say. I been a stage manager twenty-one years. You know Carol Burnett? She used to throw up every night before she went on."

"You don't understand, Martin."

"I understand very well. You're nervous? Good. Sign of a great star."

Jenny began to walk, with Martin keeping

pace. "I told Julie," she said. "I didn't think I could get through it today."

"Are you sick?"

"No."

"Then come back and sit down a while. Ten minutes, you'll feel like a different person."

"No," said Jenny, stopping once again. "Really, I appreciate what you're doing, Martin."

"Then let's go."

She shook her head. "I can't. I have too much respect for Joe Papp to go up there unprepared. I've just had other things on my mind besides work."

Martin raised his eyebrows. "They're not going to wait, Jenny," he said softly.

"I know that."

"They're going to cast that part today." He looked at her steadily. He had known her for nearly five years, and he had vast sympathy for actors and actresses; he hated to see them squander real opportunities in fits of self-destructiveness.

Jenny shrugged. "We all have our priorities," she said. "Thank you."

Martin nodded and clutched the script to his side, watching as she receded into the distance.

●   ●   ●   ●

Faye switched off the phonograph and pulled the sheet more tightly around her. Once again, she glanced at the shade, in particular at the tear near the bottom. How did Jenny live like that? she wondered. Faye imagined platoons of smirking voyeurs, stationed in shifts just outside the window. Nervous, she managed to light a cigarette and take several edgy puffs before ditching it in an ashtray. Her gaze focused on the partition that denoted the bedroom. There was a sound behind it, a telephone receiver being placed back in its cradle, and then a figure appeared in the opening to the living room.

"I'm sorry," said Leo. He zipped up his fly as he came forward.

"Forget it," said Faye.

"It was an important call."

"I'm sure."

"I *had* to take it."

Faye regarded him cynically. "It's not *taking* it that bothered me. It's *when* you took it that I felt was badly timed."

"Half my year's gross income depended on that call," said Leo.

"And half *my* year's sexual satisfaction depended on finishing what we were doing."

"Faye, please, be reasonable. The man is my biggest client."

"You mean you actually left this number?"

"Faye, I told you—"

"I changed taxis three times, made a squealing U-turn on the George Washington Bridge, and walked with a limp into the building ... and you gave out this number?"

"Faye—"

"They could've followed Michael Corleone on his way to kill Solozzo easier than someone could've trailed me, and this is the precaution you take?"

Leo came over and began to massage her shoulders. "You're so tense, Faye. You've been tense since I walked in the door."

"I'm not tense," snapped Faye. "Don't say I'm tense."

"Come on," said Leo, kneading her flesh with

his fingers. "I knew when I came in and we shook hands, things weren't going to be relaxed."

"I'm no good at this, Leo," Faye sighed. "I'm nervous. I'm clumsy."

"No, no—"

"I'm sorry about your shoes," she said, remembering the bottle of Cabernet Sauvignon she'd somehow opened onto Leo's Florsheims.

"It's just a little red wine," he said. "Personally, I think it'll do wonders for the leather, especially if the tannin content is high. Besides, the shoes are practically dry already." He bent to kiss the back of her neck. "Jesus, you're pretty."

"I'm not."

"Don't tell me you're not. I'm telling you you're pretty."

"All right, I'm pretty. I don't want to argue."

Leo extended the kisses to under her chin. "I like your perfume."

"Thank you. It may not be easy being Catherine Deneuve, but I'll tell you, it's even worse being me."

"So pretty, and sweet, and soft . . ." The kisses were descending into her cleavage.

"You've done this a lot," said Faye flatly. "Haven't you?"

"Nooo! Maybe once."

"Yeah, you've done this a lot." She paused. "Ten times? Has it been ten, Leo?" She pushed his nose away from her left nipple.

"Not ten." He nuzzled closer to the right one.

"Eight? Six?"

Leo looked up. "What is this, bingo? *A few.* That's all. A few." He began to kiss again. "But they were never important to me. *Today* is important, and only today."

"Please, Leo . . ."

Leo tugged at the top of the sheet. "I am *trying* to please Leo," he said. "And you too, if you'll let."

Faye pulled away. "A lot of meaningless affairs do not raise my appreciation of what we're doing," she sniffed. She moved to a chair across the room.

Leo looked at the ceiling. "Faye, just what is it you expected here? A virgin? I'm sorry, we're all out."

"I *expected* that my body would be considered somewhat more important than a telephone."

Leo's eyes narrowed. "Nah, nah, that's not really it, is it? It's not the phone call that's bothering you . . . it's something else."

"Tell me about it."

"I will. You know what the problem is? You don't have a good enough reason to be here." He shrugged. "Nothing to be ashamed of. You might even be lucky."

"That's what my analyst told me," said Faye quietly.

Leo stood up. "*You told your analyst?*"

"Of course."

"Jesus Christ, what did you do a thing like that for?"

"If you can't tell an analyst something like that, what's the point of having one?"

"Did you name names?" asked Leo. "Just tell me, was my actual name used in the discussion?"

"Oh, stop worrying, Leo. Everything you tell an analyst is in the strictest confidence."

"Suppose he gives it up? Suppose he becomes a grocer, or a shoe salesman? Suppose he's subpoenaed, threatened with imprisonment for contempt of court unless he turns over his files?"

"He doesn't have files, Leo. He doesn't even take notes. Half the time, I don't think he even hears what I'm telling him."

"He hears," said Leo. "And don't imagine they're all dripping with scruples. You'd be surprised the things they say at parties."

"I'll probably never see him again anyway," said Faye. "It doesn't seem to be doing me much good."

"It does good, you just have to give it time. Fifty or sixty years would definitely be helpful."

"I don't know, Leo. I just need something in my life . . ."

"And I'd give it to you," said Leo, "at least a little of it, if you'd only hold still."

"I've tried Transcendental Meditation, health foods, and jogging," said Faye wistfully. "And I am now serenely, nutritiously, and more robustly unhappy than I've ever been before."

"Because you won't relax."

"Leo, relaxation is not the answer to all of man's ills."

"But it is to yours. You overreact to everything."

"This"—Faye swept her hand around to indicate the apartment—"is not how I usually spend my lunch hour."

"You're making more out of this than it is," said Leo. "I mean, so far today it isn't anything. So you're wearing a sheet, and I haven't got a shirt—big deal." He came over and sat down next to her.

"It's not the actual *act*, Leo."

"You're his brother."

"It's the—I don't know—the gaudiness."

Leo took her hand. One thing that always distinguished him from George was that he knew when not to argue. George could move only straight ahead, assault frontally. Leo was a subject changer, a sidestepper, an attacker on the flanks. "Jesus, Faye," he said, "you are so much more interesting looking than you were eight years ago. You've got so much . . . *character* in your face."

"Why does that not overjoy me?" said Faye. "Why is life going by so fast, Leo? First I was pretty. Now I'm interesting looking with character. Soon I'll be handsome, followed by stately, then chipper, peppy, and finally—worst of all—remarkable for my age. Is that what I can look forward to: 'remarkable for her age'?"

"Why do you take such a gloomy perspective?"

"Because it's realistic."

"Gloom is the enemy of a good time."

"You're right, Leo."

Leo's face lit up. "Sure. All you—"

"I mean about my not having a good enough reason to be here. Because what I want, I can't have."

"What exactly *do* you want, Faye? Have you asked yourself that? Because if not, now's the time."

Faye smiled ruefully. "I want what Jenny has. The excitement of being in love again."

Leo stared at her, trying hard to keep the pity off his face.

"I'm so much smarter now," continued Faye. "I could handle everything so much better."

"Faye," said Leo tenderly. "Why not concentrate on the possible, instead of gifts from a genie? What's the point of tormenting yourself over something that doesn't exist? It's a dream, and maybe some day you'll have it, but right now—"

"Right now, I'm so jealous of her I could scream," said Faye. "I did for her what I wish I could have done for myself. And in return, I got her apartment in which to do exactly what I swore, when I was young and pretty, that I would never end up doing. Even when I became interesting looking with character."

"I think you're a very confused person, Faye," said Leo. "Your sentences are certainly confusing."

Faye stood up. "I've noticed that. It's what happens when you age." She started for the bedroom area. "I think you'd better leave first, Leo. I have to stay a while and practice my limp. Outside, two men will meet you and put you on a boat for Sicily, where you'll stay for five years." She disappeared behind the partition.

Leo grabbed his shirt, which had been flung over the stereo cabinet. He buttoned it carefully, then crossed to the bedroom. A slow, generalized anger was building in him, a combination of frustration, resentment, and self-pity. Faye was at the dressing table, and he spoke to her back. "At least *I'm* not a hypocrite, Faye. At least *I* know why I'm here today."

Faye concentrated on her makeup base. "Tell me about it, Leo."

"The cold, brutal truth?"

"Of course."

"Because I constantly need something new in my life. That's why I like show business. There's another opening every three weeks."

"Terrific," said Faye. She brushed on some rouge. "Wonderful, probing self-dissection . . ."

Leo ignored her. "I'm sorry, I can't be monogamous. What can I do, take shots for it? But in our system, I'm put down as a social criminal. I can't be faithful to my wife, and I hate the guilt that comes with playing around."

"But you don't hate it enough to stop . . ."

Leo smiled glumly. "No."

"And so?"

"So I compromise. I have lots of unpleasurable affairs. And what makes it worse . . . I really do care for Marilyn."

Faye started on her mascara. "If you expected me to be touched, Leo, you've miscalculated."

"I haven't calculated anything!" said Leo loudly. "I'm trying to explain something so that maybe, just maybe, you'll have a few insights of your own. As far as I'm concerned, I can't stop my behavior, and I don't expect Marilyn to understand." He inhaled. "So . . . we end up hurting each other. I don't like crawling into bed and feeling the back of a cold, angry woman."

"It didn't *have* to be that way, Leo. As I recall, I was perfectly ready—"

"But you were here under false pretenses!" shouted Leo. "You were ready for Snow White and Cinderella, for handsome princes—not Leo Schneider."

Faye looked at him in the mirror. "I wanted some affection with my sex, Leo. Is that such a terrible sin?"

"Yes," said Leo. "Yes, it is. I would love to make love to you, Faye, but that's the end of the sentence. I don't want to hurt anyone anymore. I don't want

215

the disappointments and the heartache. My needs are very simple, Faye. All I'm asking for is a little dispassionate passion."

"You *are* honest, Leo," sighed Faye. "I'll give you that. It's not as much of a virtue as people think—half the time it's accompanied by heavy doses of arrogance and self-centeredness—but it's something. It's better than being jealous."

"Jealous?" said Leo. "Why should I be jealous? Let George and Jenny handle all the romance for the East Coast. The man is half-crazed right now, and he's welcome to it. All I want in the world is a woman who looks like you and feels like you and thinks . . . exactly like me."

Faye turned and held out her hand. "Is that all there is for people like us, Leo?"

Leo took her fingers and touched them to his lips. "It can be a lot, Faye, if you look at it in the right perspective."

Faye stood up. "Leo, before you leave, would you mind giving me one warm, sincere, passionate kiss? I'll be goddamned if I'm going to go home empty-handed."

Leo drew her slowly toward him. They embraced, and their tongues intertwined. Leo's hands fluttered over her body. He pushed her toward the bed and began to claw frantically at the sheet that still encased her. "What the hell is this *tent* you're wearing?" he said in frustration as his index fingernail broke off. "Who designs your outfits, an embalmer?"

"Wait," said Faye. She began to twist and turn, and was very nearly unwrapped when she heard a gasp from the opening in the partition.

"Oh, God, I *am* sorry," said Jenny.

Faye looked around. "Oh, Jesus!"

"Oh, Christ!" said Leo.

"I should have called. I ... I didn't ... you know ... think ..." stammered Jenny. She wished very much that she could be instantaneously transported to Ecuador.

"It's all right," said Leo, feigning calmness. "It's okay. No harm done. We're all adults. It's a grown-up world. These things happen. We simply have to take a mature—"

"*Oh, shut up, Leo!*" snapped Faye.

He fell helplessly silent.

"I just came to get my summer clothes," Jenny said sheepishly. "I can do it later. I'm so sorry. Good-bye, Faye. Good-bye, Leo. Say hello to Maril—Good-bye!" She backed away and was out of the apartment.

Leo and Faye stared at each other in stunned embarrassment. "This is one of those situations in life," said Faye finally, "that a lot of people find humor in. I don't!" She stormed into the bathroom.

•   •   •   •

On the way out Jenny passed Mrs. Rose, a middle-aged neighbor from the brownstone next door. "Jenny," said Mrs. Rose, "what are you doing back here?"

"I just stopped by to pick up the rest of my things," said Jenny. She felt so disoriented, so scattered by what she'd just seen, that she wondered if her words were making any sense.

"So when do you leave on your honeymoon?" inquired Mrs. Rose.

"We've already gone," answered Jenny. "We're back."

"Back? Already? You do everything so quick. In my day we took our time, we—"

"Mrs. Rose, I'm sorry," Jenny interrupted. "I have to run. I just saw something, I don't even know what it was, but it's left me all loose and crazy. I'm sorry." She waved feebly, and started up the block.

"Too quick," hollered Mrs. Rose after her. "Slow down, you'll live longer!"

Jenny headed uptown and east, trying unsuccessfully to outpace her thoughts. After several blocks, she found herself almost running, breathless, her vision beginning to blur—and still it was no use. What machination of a diabolical God had caused her to walk in at exactly that moment? Bad enough that her best friend had to fool around, worse yet that Jenny should have indirectly assisted her—was it necessary for her to actually *see* it? Did she have to have her nose rubbed in it? And most upsetting of all, why Leo? Why someone she knew, her husband's family? How could she ever face him again, meet his wife?

She walked in a semidaze down Thirty-fourth street. After a moment, she stopped and leaned up against Macy's window. She took out a handkerchief and daubed at her eyes. From behind, a large hand seized her arm.

"Buy you a drink, lady?" came a gruff male voice.

"Get your hands off me!" shouted Jenny, whirling, prepared to lash out. And then she saw—Gus! As always, he was physically overwhelming. Handsome, rugged, manly—all the macho adjectives still applied. "Oh, Gus," she said, her voice quavering, "you scared the life out of me." For just an instant,

218

she felt an almost overpowering impulse to hug him.

"I spotted you from a bar," said Gus. He was smiling, wearing a business suit, his thick blondish hair slightly disheveled. "I chased you for two blocks. Have the Giants heard about you?"

"Thank you," said Jenny, "I would *love* to have a drink."

"Glad I asked," said Gus.

They sat in a bar on Eighth Avenue, Jenny subdued and pensive, while Gus reviewed the details of his rapidly changing life.

". . . then I was Sports and Recreation Director on the S.S. Nordholm, one of those cruise ships. I was the top 'Simon Says' man in the Caribbean."

"And now?" asked Jenny.

"I don't know. Donnie DuPree owns this bar . . . you remember him . . . he wants me to come in with him, help run the place."

Jenny looked around. "Seems to do a fairly good business."

"It's not exactly what I had planned for my life."

"I'm sorry."

"Anyway," said Gus, brightening, "you're lookin' terrific."

"Really? With puffy red eyes?"

"Your old man giving you trouble?"

Jenny shrugged and sipped her beer. "The first year's always the toughest."

"What's he do?"

"He's a writer. A novelist. His name's George Schneider."

"Never heard of him."

"That's okay," said Jenny. "He never heard of Gus Hendricks."

Gus stared at her. "Well, I hope he knows what a good thing he's got with you."

"Thanks. That's a nice thing to say."

"Hell, it's the truth," said Gus. For a moment, he choked on his Bloody Mary. "I blew a lot of opportunities in my life, but you were the best of them."

Two attractive young girls entered the bar and paused briefly as they passed Jenny's table. "Hi, Gus," said one.

"Hi, Viv," said Gus.

"When'd you get back in town?"

"A little later tonight."

The girls moved on.

"Is that one of the opportunities you *didn't* miss?" asked Jenny.

"One of the fringe benefits of my profession," said Gus. "It's hard to pass up a free lunch."

"I remember. I was cooking the dinners at the time," said Jenny.

She did remember. Always, there had been the suspicion, the unspoken accusation, the insecurity. Men in Gus's position, with his looks, attracted large hordes of admiring women. That was a 'given' in their marriage. The great uncertainty was how he would react, whether he'd have the strength necessary for self-control. Near the end, Jenny had simply preferred not to know.

"The one thing I never felt when I left was guilty," Gus said. "You're a survivor, Jen. You have that essential quality that all high school coaches look for."

"A pension?"

"Spirit."

"Let's hear it for the 'rah-rah' girl."

Gus lowered his gaze. "I miss you, Jen."

"Don't get too friendly, Gus," said Jenny quickly. "I've been traded."

"You see, I think we had it all wrong," he continued. "I should've cooked the dinners, and you should've played for the Giants. We would've made the Super Bowl."

"Well . . ." breathed Jenny. "You just gave my confidence a badly needed boost." She drained her glass. "Have you ever thought about coaching, Gus?"

He smiled ruefully. "There are plenty of coaches around. It's the talent that's hard to find."

Jenny nodded. "It was good seeing you again." She stood up. "Take care of yourself."

His eyes never left her. "You too."

Tentatively, she offered her hand, and he took it in his own. He held it quite a bit longer than necessary, her small palm lost in his meaty grip. "I suppose you want your hand back," he said hoarsely.

"I suppose so."

He let go.

"Good-bye, Gus." She turned and left, conscious that he was watching her all the way.

14

It was past three in the afternoon when she got home. She fumbled a bit with the keys—she was not yet used to the locks—pushed open the door, entered, and stood stock still. There, in the middle of the living room, was a fully-packed suitcase, George's wrinkled trenchcoat slung carelessly across it. She closed the door. George emerged from the bedroom with his attaché case.

"Hi."

"Hi."

"You had some messages," said George. He took a notepad off his desk. "I don't know if you can read my writing. Helen Franklyn called and said you had a reading for the new Tom Stoppard play Monday at ten. And Faye phoned a few minutes ago. Claimed it was urgent she talk to you, and can you have lunch with her Tuesday, Wednesday, Thursday and Friday?"

"I'm sorry," said Jenny distractedly. "What? I wasn't listening."

"Faye," said George. "Call her."

"I couldn't take my eyes off your suitcase."

George nodded. "I tried to explain everything in a letter. I left it on the bed."

"Good," said Jenny. "I was worried that I wasn't getting any mail lately. Well ... this is really something, huh? Letters, phone calls...." She broke off. "Where are you going?"

"Los Angeles," said George. "Someone at Paramount is interested in *The Duchess of Limehouse* as a film."

"When did all this come up?"

"Last week."

"Why didn't you tell me?"

George shrugged. "I had no reason to go last week."

Jenny tilted her head, acknowledging his verbal thrust. "Leave it to you to make a point clear." She moved farther into the room. "How long will you be gone?"

"I don't know."

"Where will you stay?"

"I don't know."

"Oh, come on now. You're leaving with all your luggage, but you don't know your hotel? Really .... Maybe you're just going to circle the airport for a few days?"

"You never lose your equilibrium, do you?" said George.

"You think not?"

"Doesn't seem like it."

"I'd hate to see an X ray of my stomach right now."

George sat down on the couch. "I don't think being apart for a few days is going to do us any damage."

"No worse than being together the last few days," Jenny agreed reluctantly.

"But ... if you want to get in touch with me, Leo will know where I am."

"And I'll know where Leo is."

George clapped his hands together. "I don't think I have anything else to say. . . ." He stood up.

"Me either."

"I'm glad a lot of work is coming your way. I know it's important to you. It's what you want."

"I'm glad you know what I want, George. If you'd told me five years ago, I could have saved a lot of doctor money."

"I was busy five years ago." He walked to his suitcase.

"Interesting how all this worked out, George. You pack up and go, and leave me with all your memories."

"I'm sorry," said George, "but you can't fit this size apartment in the overhead rack. And besides, they're very strict now about carry-on luggage."

Jenny shook her head. "You're just too quick for me. When it comes to words or phrases, I can't compete with you."

"Then don't."

"I'm so afraid to say anything for fear you'll cleverly twist it around to hear exactly what *you* want to hear."

"I never have to twist around anything you say," George said blithely. "It never gets that complex."

Jenny's face darkened. "Oh, God, at last! A direct confrontation. I'm not smart enough for you, is that right, George?"

"Your words, not mine."

"Well, then, go! If you're going to leave, leave! Your mystery plane is waiting to take you to your phantom hotel on the intriguing west coast. Even your life is turning into a chintzy, cheapo spy novel!" She stormed into the bedroom and slammed the door behind her.

George opened it. Something about maniacal anger fascinated him, drew him like a magnet. Genuine emotions, he told himself, were hard to find these days. The cult of cool had spread everywhere. A real, expressed feeling—even a nasty, violent one—was as valuable and rare as a silver dollar.

He watched Jenny as she stood facing the bedroom window, back to him, her shoulders quaking with the intensity of her anger, and something in his mind began to scream at his own clinical detachment. "I've got a few minutes," he said casually. "I don't want to miss what promises to be our most stimulating conversation since I mistook you for an eighty-five-year-old woman on the phone."

Jenny did not turn as he came up behind her. "Isn't it amazing," she said, "that the minute I get aggravated and abusive, it proves to be the only way I can really hold your attention?"

"I thrive on conflict," said George glibly. He heard her inhale.

"What can I say that will *really* hurt you, George? I want to send you off happy." Then she spun around suddenly and began to flail at him with her fists. She managed to land several blows on his arms and chest before he could grab her hands. He stared at her crimson, rage-twisted features.

"Are you crazy?" he said, and made the mistake of loosening his grip. She scored a hard slap to the side of his neck before he could regain control. Stung, he seized her shoulders and threw her with more force than he intended against the wall.

"I am," she moaned softly, sinking to the floor. "I am."

George glared at her. "I'll tell you something, lady. Just going is reward enough!" He stalked out.

Wondering where she got her strength, Jenny followed him into the living room. "You know what you want better than me, George. I don't understand what you expect to find out there except a larger audience for your two shows a day of suffering, but if that's how it's to be—so be it." She stood beside the couch, holding on, trying to catch her breath.

Keeping some distance between them, George eyed her suspiciously, but said nothing.

"I know I'm not as smart as you," Jenny went on. "Maybe I can't analyze and theorize and speculate on why we behave as we do, and react as we do, and suffer guilt, and love and hate. You read all those books, I don't. But there is one thing I *do* know. I know how I feel. I know I can stand here watching you try to destroy everything I've ever hoped for in my life, wanting to smash your face with my fists because you won't even make the slightest effort to opt for happiness ... and I can still be certain that I love you. That's always so clear to me. It's the one thing that sustains me. You mean so much to me I'm willing to take all your abuse and insults and insensitivity."

"Please," said George, "enough hysteria for one day . . . ."

"If you want to test me, George, go ahead and test me," said Jenny quietly.

227

"This is not a test, this is business."

"You want to leave, leave! But *I'm* not the one who's going to walk away. I don't know if I can take it forever, but I can take it for tonight, and I can take it next week. Next month, I may be a little shaky. . . . But I'll tell you something, George. No matter what you say about me, I feel good about myself. Better than when I ran from Cleveland and was frightened to death of New York. Better than when Gus was coming home at 2:00 A.M. just to change his clothes. Better than when I thought there was no one in the world out there for me, and better than the night before we got married and I thought that I wasn't good enough for you." Jenny pulled herself up straight. "Well, I am! I am wonderful! I'm nuts about me! And if you're stupid enough to throw someone sensational like me aside, then you don't deserve as good as you've got!"

Strangely, George found himself nodding in agreement. "All right," he said quietly, "you've made your point."

"I'm not finished!" declared Jenny.

"Oh . . . pardon me."

"I am sick and tired of running from people and places and relationships. I want a home, and I want a family *and* a career. I want *everything!*"

"Jenny, adults must learn to make certain compromises in life that—"

"You're missing the point! There's no harm in wanting it, George, because there's not a hope in hell we're going to get it all anyway. But if you don't *want* it, you've got even less chance than that." She paused to smooth her hair. "Everyone's looking for easy answers, and if they don't find them, they hop into different beds, hoping maybe they'll come up lucky. You'd be surprised at some of the maybes I've seen out there lately." She shook her head. "Well, none of that for me, George. If you want me, then fight for me, because I'm fighting like hell for you. I think we're both worth it. I apologize for taking up so much of your valuable time. I am now through."

She crumpled onto the sofa, exhausted.

"Tell you one thing," George said, "I'm glad you're on my side."

Jenny looked up wearily. "Do you mean it, George?"

"I didn't hear half of what you said because I was so mesmerized by your conviction."

"You mean I'm going to have to repeat it?"

George smiled. "The *idea* came through well enough. I'm not a doctor, Jenny, but I can tell you right now you're one of the healthiest people I ever met in my life."

"Funny, I don't look it."

"I want to walk over this instant, take you in my arms and say, 'Okay, we're finished with the bad part, now what's for dinner?' "

"So do it."

George shook his head. "I can't. I'm stuck, stuck someplace in my mind, glued to the floor like some big, overstuffed chair, and it's driving me crazy."

"I could rearrange the furniture."

"Don't make it so easy for me. I'm fighting to hold on to self-pity, and I run into the most understanding girl in the world." He reached down for his suitcase.

"But you're still going?"

"Yes. Maybe I can get unstuck in Los Angeles." Their eyes met. "I'll be at the Chateau Marmont Hotel."

Jenny followed him into the hall. "George!" she yelled as he reached the elevator. He pressed the button and turned.

"Couldn't I go with you? I wouldn't bother you, I would just watch."

He shook his head. "Then the people next door would want to watch, and so on and so forth, and pretty soon we'd have a crowd." The elevator doors opened, and he stepped into the car.

"If you don't call me, can I call you?" pleaded Jenny.

George shrugged. "You know, we may have one of the most beautiful marriages that was ever in trouble." The snap of the closing doors punctuated his statement.

• • • •

That night, Jenny and Faye sat near the rear of Avery Fisher Hall. The same Dutch pianist Jenny had seen with George was giving a recital.

"I have this crazy feeling," whispered Jenny, "that he's been there for weeks, that he never leaves. I picture them bringing him meals up there and then, at night, I see him going inside the piano to sleep."

"That's a very sick thing to imagine," whispered Faye. She twisted in her seat to stare at her friend.

"Please stop watching me," said Jenny, annoyed.

"I'm not watching you."

"You are!"

An elderly, well-dressed man in front of them swiveled slowly around. "Would you please shut the fuck up?" he said deliberately.

Jenny smiled and nodded.

"We don't have to stay if you don't want to," whispered Faye.

"I want to."

"Don't," advised the man.

Jenny stood up. "Come on, let's go."

Outside, they buttoned their coats against the evening chill. "They'll probably never let me in there again," said Jenny. "Imagine, exiled from Lincoln Center."

"What do you want to do now?" asked Faye. "You want to go for coffee?"

"I want to get on a plane and go to California, but I know it's the wrong thing to do." Jenny kissed Faye on the cheek. "Don't phone me. I want to keep the line open."

Before Faye could react, before she could feel insulted or lonely or *anything*, Jenny was walking rapidly away.

•   •   •   •

She had been back in the apartment only fifteen minutes when the phone rang. Please God, thought Jenny, I don't ask for much—all right, I do ask for much, but just this time?—grant me this call. After this, you can dump on me all you want. She lifted the receiver.

"Hello?"

"Hi."

"George?"

"You were expecting the Shah, maybe?"

"No, no, it's just . . . it's so quick." She rolled her eyes toward the ceiling and mouthed a heartfelt "Thank you." Into the phone, she said, "How was your trip?"

"We didn't take off yet," said George.

"What?"

"There was a bomb scare."

"But you've been there . . . my God . . . six hours already."

"They went through eight hundred pieces of luggage," said George. "It doesn't pay to pack carefully."

"You're still at the airport?"

"Unfortunately . . . yes. I'm in a booth."

"I'm sorry. Sorry you've had so much trouble."

"Don't be sorry," said George.

"Okay."

"I called Dr. Ornstein."

"And . . ."

"And we had a good talk."

"Any conclusions?"

"Yeah. He says I should travel by train. I told him I didn't need to spend twenty-five dollars to hear that."

"He charges you twenty-five dollars? For a phone conversation?"

"Sure. He says talking over the phone is no different from talking in person. Since the conversation ran less than thirty minutes, he gave me a cut-rate. He's very reasonable that way."

"So I notice," said Jenny. "If he were any more reasonable, you'd be on welfare."

There was a pause. "I just called to see if you were okay," George said.

"Yeah," said Jenny. "I'm fine. I miss you ... but I'm fine."

"Well, that's important." There was a loudspeaker announcement in the background. "Listen, that's for me. It looks like they're ready to take another crack at it, so I'll be going."

Jenny pressed the receiver to her lips. "George ... please take care of yourself. I love you very much."

"Yeah ..." he said. "Good-bye, Jen."

There was a click, and the phone went dead.

•   •   •   •

Two days later, Jenny met with Leo at Serendipity. She'd had no further word from George, though she had stayed near the phone. Finally, desperate to go out, she had called George's answering service, let them know where she'd be, then made the date with Leo. Now, at Serendipity, she sat near a window on the second floor, looking out over Sixtieth Street and hoping to spot Leo before he came in. She was startled when he sat down beside her.

"I wasn't sure I'd be able to face you again," said Leo. He signaled to the waiter. "I was going to walk in here wearing a hood."

"You don't have to explain anything, Leo ..."

"I know that."

The waiter approached their table.

"I'll have a cream cheese sandwich," said Leo.

The waiter stared at him in disgust.

"Whatsamatter, you don't have any?" asked Leo.

233

"We have," said the waiter. "Shall I hold the jelly?"

"Up to you," said Leo. "I certainly don't want it."

"More coffee?" said the waiter to Jenny.

"If you don't mind."

The waiter scurried off.

"Did you talk to Faye?" asked Leo. "What did she tell you?"

"She was completely honest and straightforward."

"Oh," said Leo glumly.

"She told me she was drugged."

Leo laughed. "I'll vouch for that."

Jenny reached in her purse and pulled out a large yellow envelope with "Leo" written on it. "I stopped by the apartment early this morning," she said. "I thought it would be a safe time. I found your wallet in the bedroom." She gave the envelope to Leo.

"You didn't have to put my name on it. It's humiliating enough." Leo tore open the envelope and quickly jammed the wallet in a rear pocket.

"Have you heard from George?" asked Jenny.

"No, but give him a couple of days. He'll figure it all out."

Jenny leaned forward. "I'm scared, Leo."

"Of what?"

"I'm so scared of losing him."

"Don't give up so soon."

Jenny swayed in her chair. "Then advise me. Tell me what to do."

"*Me?*"

"You're his brother."

"True. But this week I'm not exactly an authority on human relations."

"Was our rushing into marriage so fast a mistake, Leo?"

Leo inhaled. "The rest of his life was going to come up sooner or later."

"But maybe it was premature. . . ."

Leo shrugged. "I don't know. Things were so simple when we were kids. No matter how much trouble you got into outside, when you came home, you always got a cupcake."

The waiter returned. "Mrs. Schneider?"

"I want a cupcake," said Leo.

"A telephone call for you," said the waiter.

"Me?" said Leo.

"Are you Mrs. Schneider?"

"No."

"The call is for Mrs. Schneider."

Jenny rose. "I left a message with the service," she said. She moved toward the phone. "If it's George, Leo, the cream cheese sandwich is on me."

"How about the cupcake?"

"That too."

The phone was on a small desk at the maitre d's station. Jenny lifted the receiver anxiously. "Hello?"

Despite a faint echo, the voice at the other end was instantly recognizable. "Is that you, Bambi? It's George."

"Oh, George," said Jenny excitedly, "I'm so glad to hear your voice in one piece."

"What have you been doing?"

"Sitting around watching the telephone, mostly. Nothing good on until now." She hesitated. "How . . . how are you?"

"Dumb. A moron."

"What? Why? Your forgot something?"

"Yeah, I forgot something. When Barbara and I had a fight—and we did fight—I'd walk around the block and come back twenty minutes later feeling terrific. It was like eating Chinese food. At the airport, I said to myself, 'Of course, that's what I should do.' And that's what I did."

"You ate Chinese food at the airport?"

"I walked around the block."

"Really? You mean you actually, physically did it?"

"Yeah."

"All right, what's so dumb about that?" Jenny asked.

"I was in Los Angeles airport when I thought of it."

"Oh . . . Where are you now?"

"Wait, I'll look. Everyone's got suntans, so it must still be L.A." George paused. "I'm catching the next flight back, Jen."

"Oh, George!" She stopped, trying to keep herself from gushing. "That's . . . nice. Real nice."

"I'll be in at five-fifteen, TWA. Don't rent my room out yet. I, uh, think we have some things to clear up."

"Good or bad?"

George chuckled. "I'm a writer. Let *me* build to the climax. See you tonight." He hung up.

Jenny headed back toward the table. On the way, she passed the waiter. "Sir?"

He turned.

"Please be sure when you fill out the check to give it to me, okay? Not the gentleman."

"Yes, miss."

"Oh . . . and one more thing."

"Yes?"

"Bring an extra cupcake to the table."

•   •   •   •

At 4:45 in the afternoon, the cab was still stuck in traffic on the Van Wyck Expressway. Jenny looked at her watch, as she had five times in the past three minutes, and leaned forward. "The plane must've landed already," she said.

"Nah, they're always late," said the driver.

Jenny drummed on the seat. "Isn't there anything you can do, some other way to get there?"

The cabbie shrugged. "We could walk, but my meter ain't calibrated for that."

"Just what I needed," said Jenny. "A comedian."

"Hey . . . lady," said the driver. "Take it easy. That's how I got my ulcer. Relax and enjoy the ride."

"What ride?" said Jenny.

A half hour later, the cab pulled up in front of the TWA terminal. Jenny hopped out, flung the driver an extravagant tip, and walked rapidly into the building. "Did the five-fifteen flight from L.A. get in yet?" she asked a porter.

"Yup," said the man. "At five o'clock. They made good time."

"Damn the airlines!" said Jenny. "Where's the taxi line for arriving passengers?"

The man pointed, and Jenny was off and running before he put his finger down. Outside, in the distance, she spotted a figure entering a cab. "George!" she screamed. "George!" She raced toward him.

She fell breathlessly into his arms just as he turned. "Hey!" he said, startled. Then, softly, "Hey..." They embraced passionately, and he kissed up and down her face. "What happened, you ran from New York?"

Jenny shook her head yes, too overcome to speak. "Tell me, George," she said finally. "Just the good things. I don't want to hear the bad things."

"I never even checked into the hotel," said George. "I stayed in a motel right at the airport, and I got unstuck in the lounge."

"You did?"

"I was drinking a gin and tonic when I suddenly remembered my conversation with Dr. Ornstein. He said, whenever you feel yourself getting into trouble, ask 'What is it you're most afraid will happen *if*—' "

"If what?"

"If you do what you're scared of."

"I'm listening," Jenny said.

The cab driver gave them an impatient look.

"So I said to myself," continued George, "What is it you're most afraid will happen *if* you go back to New York, to Jenny—and start your life all over again."

"And the answer?"

"Simple. I would be happy." He kissed her again. "I have stared happiness in the face, Jenny, and I embrace it."

She stroked his hair. "Oh, George. I *love* Dr. Ornstein."

"You want this cab, or not?" the driver asked.

"Yeah," said Jenny gruffly. "He wants this cab."

"Gee," said George, picking up his suitcase as

238

she slid into the back seat, "what an aggressive lady I married."

The ride back to Manhattan took even longer than the trip to the airport, but Jenny found herself not minding at all.

"I finished the last chapter of my new book," said George as they rode on the Belt Parkway.

"Really?" said Jenny. "That's terrific! That's wonderful!"

"I did it on the plane," said George. "You want to hear it?"

"Now?"

"Why not?"

"The whole thing?"

"Well, it may not last as long as this cab ride, but it'll kill some of the time anyway." He removed a thick sheaf of papers from a leather portfolio. " 'Falling Into Place,' by George Schneider. Dedication: To Jenny, a nice girl to spend the rest of your life with." He began a new page. "Chapter One. Walter Maslanski looked into the mirror and saw what he feared most. . . ."

"Yaws?" said Jenny playfully.

"Walter Maslanski," answered George, and he hugged her as he read on.